THE SECRET LIFE OF YELLOW DOG

Danielle Sigmon

authorHOUSE®

AuthorHouse™
1663 Liberty Drive
Bloomington, IN 47403
www.authorhouse.com
Phone: 1 (800) 839-8640

Published by AuthorHouse   12/11/2015

ISBN: 978-1-5049-6084-7 (sc)
ISBN: 978-1-5049-6126-4 (e)

Library of Congress Control Number: 2015918488

Print information available on the last page.

Thank you to my husband John for all of his support. I couldn't have done this without him by my side. Also thank you to our wonderful German Shepherd Dogs Kayla, Falco and Oskar, always loyal and providing us with unconditional love.

Prologue

The Dream

Virginia tossed and turned in her bed. She'd been trying to sleep for hours but every time she finally felt herself drifting off to sleep something brought her back from the edge. Once it was an owl, hooting in the branches of the tree outside her window. Another time it was the banging and laughter of a young couple on the street below. The third time she'd jerked herself awake, having one of those strange waking dreams where she stepped off the sidewalk and woken up with her whole body jerking and her heart pounding in her chest. She rolled over, groaning slightly and resettled her pillow under her head. She glanced at the clock, sure that hours passed since she'd last looked at it but realized it was only 30 minutes later. It was only 1:00 AM.

Her mind kept racing, thinking of all the things that she accomplished that day and the things that she needed to do when she returned to work the following day. Her body was exhausted of course; she'd made sure of that. Running from office to office, up and down the stairs from floor to floor was sure to wear a person out. Not to mention the hour jog she took before dinner with her husband, Wilson. He was having no problem sleeping; she could hear him snoring in the next room. Her tossing and turning kept him awake and she eventually decided to sleep in the spare room so at least one of them could get some sleep. Misty, her Shepherd Dog, followed Virginia into the spare room and was already curled up around her feet, snoring away with her back legs twitching now and then.

All she wanted was a few hours of sleep. She'd tried everything, she drank a warm glass of milk, she counted sheep, she shifted the radio on to static, and she sat on an uncomfortable chair out in the cold. She listened to Misty's breathing and soft snuffles in the hopes that they would make her sleepy as they so often did. But none of it worked. She closed her eyes and listened to her breathing, making one last attempt at sleep. If this didn't work, she decided, she was going to have to try one of the pills the doctor prescribed her. She didn't really want to resort to medication.

Something was nagging at her, a strange feeling of anticipation and fear. She had a premonition; something was going to happen soon, something big over which she had no control. She'd had that feeling before, once or twice in her life. She smiled. The first time that she felt it was the day before she met Wilson and the second was the week before Wilson asked her to marry him. Something was coming, she knew it, but she couldn't yet tell what it was or whether it would be good or bad for her. She sighed again, taking a deep breath in and letting it out slowly.

Virginia didn't even realize that she fell asleep. One moment she was watching the back of her eyelids, the next she was in her house on The Hill looking over the land. It felt natural, right, she were exactly where she was supposed to be. She could see over all 15 acres of land, from the stream that bordered the property at the very bottom of the hill, the small wooded areas that sat in some of the dips in the countryside and the floors of the meadow, blowing in the light wind. It was cool, her skin rose with the chill of the wind as it caught her, but it was still sunny. It looked like it was spring. All of the flowers were in bloom, their colors bright and vibrant as their heads bobbed up and down. Butterflies fluttered from blossom to blossom, filling the air with even more color.

She looked around and sighed with enjoyment. She loved it here; truly, it was the happiest place in the world for her. Then she heard barking and looked around. There, bouncing in the long grass of the meadow, racing on to the shorter grass of the lawn were her Shepherd Dogs, Misty, King and Chewy. She smiled and laughed, watching them playing together. They jumped and leapt, knocking into each other, chasing each other. Even Misty was joining in and she rarely played with the other, younger dogs. They barked and whined and growled as they raced around the land. Virginia could see everything from her seat on the porch. A little part of her mind whispered to her it wasn't right, she could never see everything on her land, but she was enjoying herself too much to listen.

Then she spotted a flash of yellow from the corner of her eye, streaking across the lawn. There was a howl, of excitement not fear. And her three dogs turned and raced towards the newcomer. The yellow Labrador was met with whines of happiness and wagging tails. Chewy rubbed his face over the newcomer's, his tail wagging from side to side so hard that he was threatening to topple over at any moment. King and Misty rubbed themselves against the yellow lab, whining with joy, their tails smacking each other as they embraced their friend. Then the Labrador trotted over to Virginia and put his nose into the palm of her hand. It tickled and was slightly damp but it was warm and familiar.

"Hello Yellow Dog," she said fondly. "How are you today?"

She leaned forward and scratched behind his ears, holding his face tight and scratching around his neck and chin. Yellow Dog sat and whined, his tail wagging with sheer joy.

"Go on," she said eventually, pulling back, "Go and play with your friends, they're waiting for you."

It was true, the other dogs were waiting for Yellow Dog to join them. They were all in a line, their tails still wagging. As soon as Yellow Dog moved away from Virginia and towards them they all bounded to their feet and began to run in circles around him. They raced everywhere, backwards and forwards, tripping over each other, bumping against each other. They ran as a pack, their ears flying and their fur rippling. Their tails were always wagging, even when they were fighting with each other. It was so long since they had all seen each other, their joy filled her with happiness and she laughed as she watched them playing.

Then a colder chill washed over Virginia and the sun seemed to go behind a cloud. When she looked up and there were no clouds, the sun was still shining just as brightly. She looked back over the meadows and her lawn and everything seemed darker, the colors a little less bright than they were moments earlier. The butterflies vanished as though they were never there. The flowers faded away too, curling up like it was night time.

She spotted a smudge of darkness in the long grass, streaking towards Misty, King and Chewy. Her heart filled with dread, leaping into her throat. This newcomer was not welcome, she knew it in her gut. She was standing now, watching the scene play out. The smudge was a coyote! There was already blood on its muzzle. It faced towards King, slammed into his side and knocked him to the ground.

The coyote snarled at King, turned in a circle and glared. Its muzzle was twisted, the sharp savage teeth all showing. The growl made the hairs on the back of Virginia's neck stand on end. King whined and lay down low, Misty bounded over to help, a growl coming from her throat that Virginia never heard before. But the coyote circled her, snarling and foaming at the mouth now, and charged at her. Misty went flying through the air, landing heavily on her side among the curled up flowers. She whined pitifully, looking at Virginia with big brown eyes asking her to help. Virginia couldn't do anything; she was simply stood there, locked in place.

Chewy snarled at the coyote now, racing to stand over King's prone body to protect him. The coyote simply charged at Chewy and was moments away from sinking its teeth into Chewy's neck when a flash of yellow appeared and slammed into the feral beast. The coyote whirled away, whining suddenly. It cowered as Yellow Dog stood between it and the two dogs. Misty limped over to Chewy and King, gently licking King's neck as he climbed to his feet with a slight groan. The dogs huddled together behind Yellow Dog, their hackles raised and their muzzles twisted as they growled and snarled at the coyote. They were braver now, safer as a group and Yellow Dog's courage seemed to have emboldened them, made them realize that they could and would stand up to the coyote together if they needed to.

But it seemed like they didn't need to. Yellow Dog continued to stare at the coyote, the gazes of the two creatures locked. Then the coyote looked away, head going down. It whined in the back of its throat. Slowly, glancing at Yellow Dog the coyote backed away. It kept glancing at Yellow Dog, checking if he was still there. The coyote backed away slowly, reluctantly. Yellow Dog stepped forwards, every time the coyote took a step back, creating a bigger and bigger distance between it and his friends. Eventually the coyote turned and ran, its tail between its legs, head hanging low and a whine filling the air.

The other dogs barked and swarmed around Yellow Dog, whining and rubbing their heads against him with happiness. Virginia sighed in relief as the danger passed. The sun returned, the butterflies reappeared as if by magic. The entire area felt like it did before and she was filled with warmth. She sank into her comfortable armchair and watched her dogs and Yellow Dog all come bounding towards her.

Their claws clicked as they ran across the wooden deck. Misty, Chewy and King all settled down around the chair, lying down with groans of delights and sighing happy dog sighs. They looked like their confrontation with the coyote never happened. Not a single strand of their fur was out of place and the blood that Virginia expected to see on their fur never appeared. Yellow Dog slowly walked over, suddenly looking years older, and sat at her feet. She could feel the warm weight of him there, the movement of his rib cage as he breathed in and out. He laid his head on her knee and she rested a hand on top of it. She scratched behind his ear, the once soft fur now coarse to the touch. He was old, she realized, grey fur spotted his muzzle, his eyes and his ears. His eyes were cloudy as he looked up at her, mouth wide as he panted.

"Thank you Yellow Dog," she murmured gently. He licked her palm in understanding, "Thank you for being here to look after my babies."

Yellow Dog nuzzled against her palm and she gently rubbed along his jaw. She could hear his tail thumping on the deck. She was glad that Yellow Dog came to visit. It was perfect timing. She knew that if her dogs were alone they would never have survived the coyote's attack. Without Yellow Dog and his strange power over the coyote they would have been torn to pieces. She shivered and Yellow Dog whined, licking her hand to reassure her that everything was ok. She smiled and went back to stroking his head. He groaned with delight and rested his weight more heavily against her legs. She was happy to see him, safe and happy and right beside her.

Virginia woke up to the sun streaming through the window. For a moment she wondered where she was, forgetting that she moved bedrooms the night before. It was still earlier, at least half an hour before she usually got up but she felt well rested, as if she slept all night long. She could feel Misty stretched out on top of the duvet beside her, breathing slowly and deeply. Then Virginia remembered her sleeplessness, the tossing and turning. She was surprised that she finally managed to get to sleep and she was even more surprised that the dream hadn't woken her up or left her tired like nightmares often did.

She smiled. Dreaming of Yellow Dog, no matter how horrible the events in her dreams, always left her feeling refreshed. She had nightmares before, dreams that shifted into horrors. And then Yellow Dog would appear and everything would get better. The few times that she had nightmares without Yellow Dog there to save the day and she woke up groggy and out of sorts. That was the magic of Yellow Dog.

Virginia wondered why she was dreaming of Yellow Dog. She hadn't seen him for months, or even thought about him in over three weeks. She heard nothing from the folks on The Hill, not a single peep regarding Yellow Dog or anything else. So why the dream now?

Virginia lay back in bed, petting Misty's head as she listened to the sounds of the birds singing their dawn chorus. Yellow Dog was always a mystery to everyone who knew him. His life was a wide sprawling web that connected so many people together. He touched so many lives, made so many people happy from the young to the old, the wealthy to the poor. He was an amazing dog and no one truly realized it until a series of fateful events came to pass on The Hill.

Chapter 1

A City Dog

"Hey Janie!" Amanda shouted, "Have you seen those blue shoes Eric loves?"

"No," Janie shouted back, "Last time I saw them they were on your bedroom floor,"

"I know," Amanda called back, "That's where I left them before my shower. Now they're gone."

Amanda walked through the apartment, the sounds of the city outside floating in through the open window. She was dressed to the nines, every hair in place and make up done perfectly. Her soft blue dress floated around her legs as she walked across the hard wood floor bare foot. She spotted Janie on the sofa, no makeup and hair pulled back, clad in comfortable tracksuit bottoms and a loose white t shirt. She was reading one of the many magazines that littered Amanda's coffee table.

"Why not wear the black shoes?" Janie asked, glancing at her, "They make your legs look amazing."

"They don't look right with this dress," Amanda said as she perched on the edge of the sofa, "I tried them on earlier but the blue shoes were the only ones that looked right."

A soft growl came from the kitchen. Both women turned to look and Amanda's jaw dropped.

"What is that thing doing with my shoes?" she cried.

She rushed over to the kitchen but she was too late to save her blue shoes. Soft blue suede littered the tiled floor and the black soles, complete with extra padding, were now a chewed mess. Amanda knelt down and tried to pull one of the soles from the mouth of the pale yellow puppy that sat there with its tail wagging. The puppy growled and pulled back.

"No!" Amanda shouted, "Drop it!"

The puppy growled happily and its tail wagged harder. It stood on its little legs and pulled back, jerking as Amanda managed to drag it across the floor, its claws scratching.

"Bailey!" Janie shouted when she saw the mess that her dog made, "Bailey drop it!"

The puppy dropped the sole and quickly ran over to sit by Janie's feet, his tail wagging so hard that he shook with every movement. Amanda knelt down and picked up the pieces of her favorite shoes.

"No!" she wailed, cradling them in her hands, "Yuck they're all soggy! These were my favorite! That thing is a monster!"

"He's only a baby," Janie murmured as she picked Bailey up. The dog licked at her face, "He doesn't know any better. He just thought they were toys."

"He's torn them to pieces!" Amanda cried, "They were limited edition and cost me $500!"

"Well you said they always pinched anyway," Janie said helplessly, "Maybe it's better he tore those up. At least he didn't pee on your sofa this time."

Amanda glared at her friend for a moment before sighing. She turned and walked away.

"I'm going to have to go with the black shoes now!" she called back, "Eric doesn't like those nearly as much."

***

Dinner was going well, the conversation was flowing and so was the wine.

"He really peed on your sofa?!" Eric cried out through a roar of laughter. "What did you do?"

"I threw it out," Amanda said, "The cleaners couldn't get it clean even after three attempts. They tried everything they knew and still no luck. I ended up getting a new leather one."

"Well at least if it pees again it'll just wipe clean," Eric said with a shrug. "Now, enough about the little yellow monster pretending to be a dog. What do you want to do after desert?"

"I can think of a few things," Amanda said with a smile.

I'm just a love machine! The sound of Amanda's phone ringing startled her and she spilled wine on her hand in surprise. She scrambled for her bag and began searching through it.

"I'm sorry I thought I put it on silent," she said as the song continued to play. "I told everyone to leave me alone, I don't know why anyone's calling me"

She looked at the name on the screen and frowned. After a moment's pause she accepted the call and put the phone to her ear.

"Janie?" she said, "This better be important, I told you not to call me until I text you,"

"I'm sorry," Janie said from the other end, "I know you wanted to be left alone."

She sniffled slightly and Amanda sat up straighter.

"Janie," she said quietly, "Janie what's wrong?"

"It's my mom and dad," Janie said with a small sob, "there's been an accident."

"Oh my goodness," Amanda said, "Are they ok?"

"No," Janie said, crying a little louder now, "They're really hurt. They've got to stay at the hospital for a while."

"Oh Janie," Amanda said softly, "I'll be there as soon as I can."

Amanda ended the call and dropped the phone on the table with a sigh. She put her head in one hand and sipped at her wine with the other.

"I'm sorry, I'm going to have to go," she eventually said. "There's an emergency with my friend."

"I heard," Eric said quietly, "Do you want me to come with you? Is she ok?"

"Her parents were in an accident," Amanda said even as she climbed to her feet and started to put things in her bag, "You're probably better off going home and relaxing, there's not much more you could do. There'll be a lot of crying and wailing. I think it's a bit early in the relationship for you to be helping with that yet."

Eric chuckled. Amanda stood and leaned over the table to kiss Eric gently on the lips.

"I'll call you," she said quietly against his lips.

She turned and left, pausing to allow the maître d to help her into her coat.

***

Amanda let herself into Janie's apartment and was met by Bailey barking at her feet. She took her shoes off and placed them on top of the cupboard beside the door, well out of reach of the small yellow monster pretending to be a dog.

"Janie," Amanda called out as she hung up her coat. "Janie! Are you ok?"

Amanda walked through her friend's apartment, the puppy close on her heels. She paused in the doorway and gasped as she saw her friend. Janie was still in her comfortable clothes but she was now curled up on the sofa, surrounded by used tissues and sobbing into a cushion. Amanda rushed over to her friend, dropping her bag on the floor with no concern as to where it lay. She wrapped her arms around Janie and pulled her close. She ran her hand over Janie's head and rocked her gently. Janie started crying harder and harder and clutched at Amanda's shoulders so hard that Amanda couldn't help but wince slightly.

After some time passed the crying stopped. They sat there for a moment, wrapped around each other. Amanda pulled away with a sigh after Janie's shaking stopped completely.

"What's happened?" she asked quietly. "Did you find out anything else?"

"They were on the highway," Janie said, her voice catching, "A truck carrying a bunch of cars lost control and raced across the intersection. It toppled over and crashed into their car. Then some of the cars that were on top of truck fell off and hit their car as well. They were unconscious when the ambulance took them away but they were in surgery the last time that I heard."

"Oh Janie!" Amanda gasped, "How bad is it?"

"My dad broke his spine." Janie said, the tears starting once more, "The doctor said it should heal eventually but he's going to need a lot of physical therapy and he's going to be in a wheelchair for the rest of his life probably."

"And your mom?" Amanda asked, "Is she badly hurt?"

Amanda held her breath, waiting for an answer. She loved Janie's mum, absolutely adored her. Whenever she visited Janie at her parents' house she felt a part of the family. She hoped, desperately, that things weren't as bad as they sounded.

"Her leg was crushed," Janie said eventually, "The passenger side door slammed into it and broke her femur in two places. Her right arm is broken and she's shattered her collar bone. Then there's the massive concussion and cheek fracture."

"So…" Amanda said slowly, "What's going to happen? I mean, they're both pretty much helpless and will need some help. Are they getting a live in nurse or something?"

"They're going to need 24 hour care, at least until my mom's healed up a little more," Janie said with a sigh, "The hospital bills alone are going to cost them a small fortune as it is, there's no way they're going to be able to afford to pay for a nurse on top of the physical therapy bills and medication. So… I'm going to move to live with them until they're better,"

"How long will that take?" Amanda asked, already starting to guess a rough time frame.

"The doctors don't know yet," Janie said, sobbing slightly again, "It could be anything from six months to six years until they're able to at least look after themselves enough."

"When are you leaving?"

Janie just looked at her friend and shrugged. Amanda smiled at her weakly.

"As soon as I can," Janie said. "I'm putting the apartment up for a sublet and my landlord's going to put everything into storage for me."

"Tonight then?" Amanda asked, "Shouldn't you wait until the morning? It's going to be hard to drive when you're like this; you can barely see your eyes are so swollen."

The friends sat in silence for a while, Amanda reaching out to take Janie's hand which she held it tightly.

"There's something I need you to do for me," Janie said eventually, breaking the silence. "And I don't think you're going to like it. But I need you to do it. I'm not going to be able to focus on helping my parents if I'm left worrying about this."

Amanda sat there, waiting for Janie to ask. A small knot of dread began to build in her stomach as she thought through what Janie could ask. She already had an idea but she really hoped that she was wrong. She didn't want to hear it but she knew she would.

"Will you take Bailey?" Janie asked after the moment of silence stretched and stretched.

Amanda closed her eyes and sighed. She really didn't want that to be the question.

"I know it's a lot to ask," Janie said quickly, taking Amanda's silence for refusal, "I know you're really busy and you're not exactly fond of him but I can't bear the thought of putting him into a pound. I'd feel so much happier if you took him and looked after him. I might be able to take him back eventually but I have no idea when and I need to know he's somewhere safe and he's happy."

"Janie…" Amanda said slowly and sadly, shaking her head gently, "I don't have the time to look after a dog. Heck I don't even know how to look after a dog. Are you sure there's no one else you could ask?"

"There's no one else I trust," Janie said firmly, "Everyone would probably say yes when I asked but the moment I get out of the city they'd probably put him in the pound. I need you to do this. I wouldn't ask if it wasn't important, believe me."

Amanda sat there, thinking. She watched as Bailey lay on the rug in front of the fake fireplace in Janie's living room. For a moment she could picture Bailey doing the same in her own apartment and thought that maybe things wouldn't be so bad. Then she looked at Janie and saw the look of love on her face as her friend stared at the dog. Amanda knew there and then that there was no way she could refuse. It would break Janie's heart losing the dog and that was the last thing that Amanda wanted to do.

"OK," Amanda said, "I'll look after him. Only because it's you, if it were anyone else I'd have said no!"

"Oh thank you," Janie cried out, throwing her arms around her friend. "Thank you, thank you, thank you."

***

A few hours later Amanda let herself into her apartment and dropped Bailey's lead. She dumped the bag of dog supplies on the table in her hallway and sighed. Bailey already ran off, dragging his lead around as he explored his new home.

"Bailey, get back here you stupid dog," she called, "You've still got your lead on you fool. You'll get stuck on something."

She kicked off her shoes and raced after the dog. Bailey clearly thought that it was all a game and started to race away from Amanda, waiting until he was almost caught before he raced away again. Now for the first time since leaving Janie's apartment Amanda wondered how she had gotten into this mess. Within moments of agreeing to take Bailey Janie started shoving things into a bag and into Amanda's arms. The goodbye was tear-filled and Bailey whined and whined as Janie hugged him over and over. He knew that something was going on but had no idea what. He was unhappy as Amanda had led him out of the building and into the street. He kept pulling at his lead as they made their way down the stairs and once or twice attempted to pull free to race back to Janie's home. He continued to pull even when they were outside on the street. No taxis would take them and Amanda and Bailey were forced to walk 30 blocks to get back to Amanda's apartment.

Now she was stuck racing around the apartment trying to get the lead off her new dog. Her phone rang, Eric's name popped up on the screen and she answered even as she continued to chase him around.

"Hello," she said, out of breath,

"Hey…" Eric said slowly. "Are you ok?"

"Yeah," she said as she panted for breath, "Why?"

"You raced off to see your friend because something bad happened," Eric pointed out, "And now you sound like you're running around or…"

"Oh yeah," Amanda said. "Sorry, it's not what you think. Janie's going back to live with her parents and help them until they can look after themselves again."

"So why are you out of breath?" Eric asked,

"I sort of have a new dog," Amanda said as she finally caught hold of the lead, "Stay still Bailey, I need to get this off,"

"Bailey!" Eric cried out, "Isn't Bailey the name of that dog you were moaning about earlier?"

"Yeah about that…" Amanda said. "I told Janie I'd look after him until she can get back to Rochester and take him back."

"Oh Amanda…" Eric said with a sigh. "How do you get yourself into these messes?"

"If I knew that I wouldn't get i- No!" Amanda broke off, "Bailey no! That's the kitchen, don't pee there."

Amanda dropped the phone and raced over to the kitchen where Bailey was peeing, his tail wagging and staring right at her as he peed. Eric's laughter came through the phone as she left it lying on the sofa.

***

"Oh god no," Amanda said with a moan as she stepped through her front door. "Bailey, why can't you go on the newspaper?"

She closed the door behind her and stepped around the small piles of brown material that Bailey left all over her floors. Her heels clicked as she walked over the hard wood. There was no sign of the dog anywhere. She walked through the apartment, seeing no hint of the yellow dog. As she checked each room she wondered what trouble Bailey had gotten into this time. For the past few weeks she'd had all sorts of trouble on Bailey's part. The landlord had called her several times due to Bailey's barking all day, he'd managed to gnaw through a water pipe which led to flooding in the apartment below. Bailey could not be left alone for too long in the apartment.

Amanda heard a ripping sound coming from her bedroom and raced towards it. She threw open the door and whimpered as she took in the destruction that the small yellow animal left in its wake. There were feathers everywhere, covering her bed and floating through the air. Her duvet was rumpled and slightly stained. And there, in the middle of her bed, was Bailey. His tail wagged and he barked as he caught sight of Amanda. A pillow case was hanging from his mouth and he was surrounded by bits of pillow.

"Well done boy," Amanda said with a sigh, "You successfully killed my pillows."

She walked over and reached out towards Bailey. He trotted over the duvet, bouncing on the mattress and shoved his head against her hand. She smiled softly and scratched him behind the ears.

"What am I going to do with you?" she said with a sigh.

She sat on the edge of the bed, checking around for any more disgusting stains. Bailey wiggled closer and leaned against her as she continued to stroke his fur. She truly did enjoy having him around but she wasn't home enough to give him the attention that he needed. She worked all day and most nights she was out on dates, with friends or networking with various clients.

"I think it may be time to look for a new owner," she said gently, "I know you like it here and I like having you here but it might be better for you to go somewhere else."

Bailey whined and nuzzled closer to her. Amanda sighed and picked him up. She was going to stay at Eric's place that night so there was no need to clean up the room. She carried Bailey out into the living room and settled on to the sofa. Bailey barked happily and stepped around her, almost falling off the sofa a time or two. Amanda laughed and played with Bailey.

She wished she could keep him, she'd tried to keep him and make sure he was happy, just like Janie asked. But it was getting harder and harder to do. She didn't have enough time to give him and he didn't get enough attention to keep himself amused. It wasn't fair to him, left alone and bored all day in the apartment and it wasn't fair to Amanda to have her days and nights disturbed by a bored and restless puppy. Then the phone rang.

"Hey Amanda!" Janie's voice said down the line, "How are things?"

"They're ok," Amanda said quietly. "You sound a little happier. Are things ok at your end?"

"Mom and Dad are doing much better," Janie said happily, "They're out of intensive care and in the general care ward now. They might even be able to come home within a few weeks if all goes well."

"That's great!" Amanda cried, hugging Bailey closer as he almost fell off the sofa again, "Maybe you'll be able to come back sooner than you thought,"

"I'm afraid not," Janie said after a moment's pause. "The thing is… I think I'm going to stay here."

"What?" Amanda asked, "You're staying with your parents from now on?"

"I'm moving back in with them yes," Janie said firmly, "I like having so much space compared to the city and it's such a slower speed of life. The doctors say they're going to need help for a long while yet and I sort of… met someone…"

"Well that's …." Amanda said hesitantly, "That's… great!"

"I know," Janie said, "I wasn't looking for it but it just sort of happened."

"So… when are you coming to get Bailey?" Amanda asked quickly, "I mean if you're staying there and there's so much more room then maybe you could have Bailey live with you. I bet your parents would love him,"

"I would but…" Janie said, again pausing, "I don't think I can look after both Bailey and my parents. He needs loads of attention and I'm going to have my hands full with my parents. It wouldn't be fair to him,"

Amanda sighed softly.

"What's wrong?" Janie asked, "Amanda?"

"It's Bailey," Amanda said quietly, "I love having him with me but it just isn't fair on either of us,"

"He's still causing problems then?" Janie asked, "I thought it might just be because he was struggling to get used to a new home. I hoped things would settle down soon."

"So did I," Amanda said, "He's just restless and I don't have enough time to give him the attention he deserves,"

"It's not fair on either of you," Janie said, sighing heavily, "What do you want to do?"

"I don't know…" Amanda said quietly.

Bailey barked and licked Amanda's face. She giggled and hugged Bailey close.

***

A few weeks later Amanda was at her wits end. Bailey was barking non stop whenever she wasn't in. The neighbors complained and the landlord was threatening to evict her if she didn't get Bailey under control. She'd come home several times to find pillows and cushions and shoes completely destroyed by Bailey's chewing and the sofa was peed on more times than she could count. In fact her entire apartment smelled like dog urine now. She didn't know what to do and as always she turned to her parents.

"Hey ma," she said when her mother picked up, "How are you?"

"Amanda! Darling!" Diane cried, "Everything's wonderful here and we're all doing really well. Your dad loves living here and Shadow has plenty of yard to run around"

That was when a light bulb went off in her head.

"Mom…" she said slowly, "Would you be willing to take on another dog?"

"What?" Dianne asked in confusion, "Why would you be wondering that?"

"I have a dog," Amanda said, "But things aren't working out and I really can't take him to the pound."

"Why did you get a dog if you can't look after it?" Diane asked,

"I didn't think it through really," Amanda explained. "I took him because Janie asked me. I love him we just can't seem to make it work."

"Why did Janie ask you to look after her dog?" Diane said "Can't she look after him?"

"Her parents were in a car accident," Amanda said. She heard Diane gasp and continued quickly, "They're out of the woods now but they're going to need a lot of looking after."

Amanda continued to explain the situation to her mother and when her father returned they were both on speaker phone. She was forced to explain the situation again and ask them if they could take Bailey on at their home. They had room, there was no doubt about it. They already had a dog and knew how to make sure that a dog was happy and well looked after. They could give all the attention to Bailey that he needed.

But her parents were still unsure. Their dog, Shadow, was old and quite mean. They were worried about how he would react to a new dog in his territory. Amanda was forced to plead with them, beg them to take Bailey because she didn't want to lose him completely and she didn't want to let Janie down. If her parents wouldn't take Bailey she would be forced to put Bailey in the pound and that was the last thing she wanted to do. It would break Janie's heart and make her worry more than she already was. She explained all of this to her parents in a last ditch attempt to get them to agree.

And when they heard all of that, heard how worried Janie was about Bailey being in a good home and how much Amanda loved Bailey they agreed. Amanda could hear their concern in their voices. They weren't sure how well Shadow would take a new dog in his life. Amanda hoped that everything would be ok, she needed everything to be ok.

Chapter 2

A Country Dog

The drive up to the country town where Amanda's parents lived was a long one. It was sad too. Amanda got Bailey into her car fairly easily. He'd ridden in the car a few times to go for long walks they took in the parks just outside of the city. But today he knew something was different. His tail wagged when Amanda opened the front passenger seat to let him jump in. It was still wagging a half hour later when they were well past their usual walking places. His head was out of the window, tongue flying as he enjoyed the feeling of the wind on his face, running through his fur. It was only a little while later when he began to realize that there was something wrong and the drive wasn't going as usual.

He started to whine and shifted in the passenger seat, moving away from the window to be closer to Amanda.

"It's ok boy," she said quietly when he nuzzled her hand and licked it gently. "We're going on an adventure."

She sniffed, fighting back tears that were threatening to spill down her face. Bailey seemed to know that she wasn't telling the whole truth and shifted closer. He nuzzled against her face. Amanda lifted her hand to gently scratch behind his ears.

"I know baby," she murmured, "I know this is scary. But you're going to live on a big farm where you'll have all the room that you want to run around and play."

Her voice threatened to crack, the tears beginning to slowly slide down her cheeks. Bailey's wet, warm tongue licked the salty water away and he continued to whine. Amanda's heart was breaking. She loved Bailey, really she did but she knew that keeping him in the small city apartment, shut away for long hours with no room to play and run around. It wasn't fair on either of them to keep him in the city. But those facts still didn't make what she was doing any easier.

"Hey," Amanda said, faking happiness, "You'll like it there. Ma and Pop are going to be around all day, there to play with you and take you for long walks. You can run around on their farm, through the fields and stuff."

Bailey yipped lightly, moving back in his seat and looking at Amanda. She was sure that the yellow Labrador was really listening to her and taking in everything that she was saying.

"And you know what else?" Amanda said. Bailey yipped like he wanting to know, "You'll have someone to play with! Ma and Pop have a dog of their own and they'll let you play with him. He can be a bit mean but I know that you'll get him to like you and you'll have everyone wrapped around your little finger within weeks,"

Bailey panted and his tail wagged again happily. He put his head out of the window again. Amanda looked at him and smiled. Maybe things weren't as bad as they seemed.

"I'll be able to come visit you!" she said after a few more minutes passed, "Ma and Pop are always going on at me to come and see them more and now I'll have to come so I can see you. You know what? I bet that's why they agreed to take you. They're sneaky like that."

Bailey looked at her, his head turned and cocked to one side so that he could watch her as she spoke. When she was done he barked again and turned back out of the window. Amanda smiled and went back to focusing on the driving.

***

"I'm worried about Shadow," Diane said suddenly, "What if he doesn't like the new dog?"

She and her husband Henry sat at the breakfast table, following their usual morning routine. Shadow sat by the door, looking out over their fields and watching the horses running and prancing in the spring morning sun. Diane and Henry were just waiting for Amanda to arrive.

"That's something we'll have to deal with when they get here," Henry said, not looking up from the newspaper that he was reading, "Shadow's a mean dog, we both know it, but we've spoiled him. It's about time he learned to play better with others,"

"I caught him chasing the little bay foal yesterday evening," Diane admitted. Henry looked up at her sharply, concern appearing quickly on his face, "The one that I was walking around the paddock in the afternoon. I went out to check on the horses before I went to bed and I caught him racing around after her."

"That dog's a jealous hound," Henry said as he shook his head. "Any time we give attention to an animal that isn't him he goes mad. We need to figure out how to change it."

"What if he goes after Bailey?" Diane said, her voice full of concern, "Amanda will be so upset if he's hurt, not to mention Janie's heart would break if she found out he'd been hurt,"

"We'll manage darling," Henry said, and sighed. "We'll do like we always do and manage."

The couple lapsed into silence, each wrapped up in their own thoughts and fears. Time passed and then suddenly they heard the sounds of a car engine as it drove up their driveway. Amanda had arrived.

***

"Look at all that room!" Amanda cried out as they pulled to a stop outside of her parents' house. "So many fields to run around in for you."

Bailey barked and looked at her again. He panted and his mouth hung open. He was smiling and she laughed before turning off the engine. She climbed out of the car and stretched. She groaned as her muscles moved and shifted, finally free from their cramped positions. She walked around the car and opened the door to let Bailey out.

Before the dog had a chance to jump out another dog raced around from the side of the house. It was barking loudly, bounding over the earth at a startlingly fast speed. Amanda was barely able to make out the dark brown form of the German Shepherd as it raced towards her and her car.

"Shadow!" Amanda heard Pop shouting. "Shadow get back here!"

The dog, Shadow, ignored Henry's shouts and continued towards the car, Amanda and Bailey. Amanda cried out and scrambled into the passenger seat, shoving Bailey further into the car. She reached for the car door and slammed it closed. Seconds later the car rocked as Shadow slammed into its side. There was a scrambling of claws on metal as Shadow leapt and jumped at the window. He barked and snarled at the newcomers, intent on seeing the danger to his family off. Amanda cried out again as Shadow's muzzle pressed against the glass. She looked towards the side of the house and sighed in relief as she saw her father racing around the corner. Bailey barked happily at the strange dog, wanting to play with his new friend. He scrambled into the back seat and stood there, barking at the other dog. Shadow moved along the car to bark and snarl at the invader.

Henry ran over and grabbed at Shadow's collar. He wrestled the irate dog away from the car. Moments later Diane appeared through the house's front door, a strong leather lead in her hand. She raced over towards Henry and Shadow who were wrestling with each other a few yards away from the car. She ducked and dodged Shadow's snarling mouth before she eventually clipped the lead in place and backed away. She held the end of the lead tightly as Henry finally let Shadow go. Her arms jolted and were yanked as Shadow leapt away from his owners, intent on getting back towards the car. Henry jumped forwards and took hold of the lead. He began to lead the dog back around the house, arms straining as Shadow pulled and tugged. Bailey leapt back into the front seat, climbing into Amanda's lap to try and reach his new friend. As Shadow was dragged around the side of the house Bailey raced over to the driver's seat and stood there barking. His tail wagged rapidly and hit Amanda in the face.

When Shadow was out of sight Diane walked over to her daughter's car and opened the passenger door. Amanda climbed out and wrapped her arms around her mother.

"Is he always like that?" she asked when they broke apart.

"I'm afraid so," Diane said with a sigh, "You should see him when the post man arrives,"

The two women looked at each other.

"The retirement seems to be treating you well," Amanda said eventually, "You look happy,"

"Oh I am," Diane said with a sigh. "Your father and I love it out here on The Hill,"

"The Hill?" Amanda asked, "I didn't know the farm had a name."

"Oh it doesn't" Diane said, "I'll tell you all about it later. Let's just get this little guy out so he can stretch his legs."

"Oh gosh!" Amanda cried.

She spun around and leaned into the car to grab Bailey's lead. She clipped it onto the dog's collar and tried to pull him away from the driver's seat. He stood there, looking after his new friend and desperate to get back to him. Eventually Amanda managed to get Bailey out of the car and onto the driveway after a lot more pulling on the lead. Bailey leapt down and turned around and around. His tail wagged wildly and his nose twitched as he explored the smells of his new surroundings.

"Isn't he beautiful?!" Diane cried.

She stepped forward and knelt down beside the yellow Labrador. He twisted and turned and butted against her. Diane scratched behind his ears and rubbed all over his coat. He barked and his entire body shook with happiness as he enjoyed this new attention.

"Come on," Diane said. She stood up straight and groaned as her joints ached. "We'll go out to the paddock so he can have a run around."

Amanda went to follow her mother but paused and turned back to her car. She needed to get Bailey's things from the trunk of her car.

"Your father will get those," Diane said dismissively, "Come on. You need to see the farm for yourself."

The two women walked around the side of the house and Amanda gasped as she saw the true size of her parents' new home for the first time. Henry and Diane bought the country house a few years before when they finally retired and decided that it was time to move out of the city. The house and its surrounding fields were on the outskirts of a small town, an hour and a half outside of Rochester. Amanda had not visited them since they relocated, her life too busy with work, dating and socializing to spare the time to visit her parents who were now living a slower pace of life out in the country, away from everything.

"It's amazing," Amanda eventually said, "I can't believe that you found it,"

"I know," Diane said with a small smile. "I almost wish we'd moved here sooner. Then again we wouldn't be enjoying it as much."

Amanda laughed and helped her mother open the gate to the paddock. They walked through and pulled the gate shut behind them. In the small area of grass, surrounded by fences, Amanda felt safe enough to remove Bailey's lead and let him run around. The two women watched as Bailey raced around and sniffed at the grass.

"So what do you do out here?" Amanda asked, looking around. "It's pretty quiet I bet,"

"Oh it is," Diane said with a happy sigh.

They looked out over the fields around them. In a dip further down the hill was a collection of houses. Amanda could see the line in the trees that marked the road. A few buildings were visible among the trees.

"The horses keep us fairly busy," Diane said eventually, "We try to exercise them every day and most of the time we let them out into the fields so each evening we have to round them up and get them back in the stables again. The rest of the time we play cards with friends."

"Didn't Dad say something about painting?" Amanda asked, "I'm sure that he mentioned it a few months ago,"

"Oh yes!" Diane cried, "I give painting lessons here at the house. It keeps me nice and busy and I get to meet such interesting people."

"So you're happy then?" Amanda asked, concern in her voice, "Really happy?"

"Very happy," Diane said with a wide smile, "Everything is wonderful for us. And it will be for Bailey too."

***

Life for Bailey on The Hill wasn't as wonderful as Diane hoped. He was a wonderful dog and she and Henry loved him deeply. Within hours of Amanda driving back to Rochester the little dog made himself at home in their country house. Henry came in from tying Shadow up outside and joined Diane and Amanda in their conversations. Bailey instantly sat at his feet and put his head on the man's knee. He whined, begging for a scratch and Henry obliged him. Eventually it was time for Amanda to leave and he tried to get into her car with her. He whined as Henry held him back but he hadn't pulled. For a while after Amanda's leaving Bailey moped on the couple's front porch but Henry managed to get him interested in a game of fetch. Bailey's enjoyment of the game and lively puppy energy made the couple laugh within moments and as the sun went down they brought Bailey inside and set him up with a bed in the corner of the sitting room. He'd woofed down the food they put out for him and lapped up the water from the bowl that had his name printed on it.

Things went very wrong later that evening. Henry made sure Shadow calmed down before he brought him inside. But Shadow wasn't calm. He was furious and as soon as Henry released the dog's lead he started barking and snarling at Bailey. At first the yellow dog barked and wagged his tail in the air, bouncing around ready to play. But Shadow had kept snarling and barking and eventually Bailey had backed away. He'd ended up cowering in the corner, whining pitifully. Diane and Henry were heartbroken but still hopeful that things would improve and their two dogs would get along.

But Shadow was determined that they wouldn't get along. Whenever he was in the house he stayed close to one of his two owners and chased Bailey away whenever he got too close. This caused more problems for Diane than Shadow knew. His determination to keep anyone away from his owners also included people, not just Bailey. Whenever

Diane's students came around to her house for a painting lesson he would bark at them, jumping up and snapping whenever they got too close to her. Some of the students never returned. Others were dog owners and suggested that it was jealousy and the upset at having a new dog in the house that was making Shadow act like that. Henry agreed and the couple tried to figure out what they could do to ease their lives.

"I just don't like the idea of Bailey getting hurt," Diane said sadly, "He's so small and just doesn't realize that he needs to stay away from Shadow. He only wants to play,"

"I know my love," Henry said. He put his arm around Diane's shoulders and was met by a growl from Shadow, "Oh hush you fool. I'm hugging my wife."

Shadow fell silent and settled his head back on top of his paws. The click of dog nails on wooden floors reached their ears and Shadow lifted his head up. He began to growl softly as he stared at the doorway. Bailey slowly came around the corner, whining softly as he stepped into the sitting room where the rest of his new family was assembled.

"Shadow…" Henry said warningly, "Shadow! Down!"

Shadow had climbed to his feet and his growling grew in volume. He looked at Henry, still growling.

"Shadow!" Henry shouted, "Sit!"

Although Shadow didn't want to follow the command he was still loyal to his master so he sat. He didn't stop growling through and kept shifting his front paws as Bailey slunk through the room. The younger dog walked over to the sofa where Henry and Diane were settled and licked at Diane's hand. Shadow barked but quickly fell silent again at a command from Henry. Diane gently rubbed Bailey's head, playing with his big floppy ears. Bailey's mouth dropped open and his tongue fell out. He laid his head against Diane's leg and closed his eyes. He groaned in happiness and his tail began to wag wildly. Shadow growled gently but settled down. Bailey continued to receive rubs from Diane and Shadow rose to his feet.

Henry watched warily, waiting for the dog to go after Bailey. Instead Shadow walked over to sit beside Henry and copied Bailey's posture. For a moment Henry froze in surprise. This dog never came and demanded a cuddle from his owners but now he was. Shadow's tail wasn't wagging and Henry wondered whether the older dog was just doing it to try and get a rise from Bailey. He eventually started rubbing at Shadow's ears, stroking the soft fur of his neck. At first Shadow was tense and his eyes were fixed on Bailey. Slowly, as the petting continued, Shadow relaxed, his eyes drooped closed and his tail began to wag softly.

"Well would you look at that?" Diane said quietly, "I have never seen him like that before,"

"I know!" Henry said. He shifted and knocked Shadow who opened his eyes for a moment before settling his head on Henry's knee once more and accepting more stroking. "I guess he likes it more than he expected. "Eh boy?"

Shadow made no sound. Instead he just settled his weight more heavily against the man's leg and wagged his tail harder.

***

After that night things were a little easier between the two dogs. It was as though Shadow realized that the two of them could share their owners, that there were enough owners who could give them both as much attention as they each desired. Shadow wasn't completely happy and from time to time, particularly when the temperature got quite high, he would snap whenever Bailey got too close to Diane or Henry. On those days Bailey would disappear into the fields surrounding the house, sometimes hiding among the horses or exploring the clusters of woods that lay in the area. He would often return home tired and thirsty, covered in mud.

It was night time that was the most difficult for Diane and Henry. Shadow liked to sleep at the foot of their bed, sprawled out by the couple's feet. Once or twice Bailey tried to join them and Shadow would snarl and snap until the younger dog left the room with his tail between his legs. Diane attempted to alternate the nights spent with the two dogs but Shadow would have none of it. The first time they tried to shut Shadow out so Bailey could sleep on their bed the German Shepherd scratched at the door and whined. Henry had eventually tried to put Shadow outside but he began to howl until the couple gave up and let Shadow back into their bedroom. Bailey was forced to sleep in his own bed in the sitting room.

They thought that was the end of the argument between the two dogs but it was only the beginning. One evening they left them both in the house alone in order to go and play cards with their friends. When they returned they found their sitting room in ruins and Bailey cowering in their pantry.

"I don't know what to do," Henry said with a sigh as they cleaned up the mess. "We can't keep on like this,"

"I know," Diane said, resting her head on her husband's shoulder, "They're ok when we're here but the moment we disappear from their sight Shadow starts going for him."

"What should we do?" Henry asked, "Do you want to get rid of Bailey, find him another family to live with?"

"No!" Diane said sharply, "He's already gone through so much and had so many families. He deserves some stability. Besides, I love him too much to give him up now,"

In the end Bailey took it upon himself to solve the couple's problem. He knew that there was something wrong with his new family and that he and Shadow were at the center of it. He could also tell that the problem got worse when it was night time and Shadow was trying to get him away from the couple's bed. So he decided to sleep outside.

"Is he ok?" Henry asked from his seat on the bed.

Diane was at the window, peering into the darkness outside. She could make out Bailey's sleeping form under the tree at the bottom of the garden.

"I think so," she said eventually, "He doesn't seem to be upset or anything."

"Maybe he likes sleeping out there," Henry said quietly, "It's probably nice and cool out there. Might even be nicer than sleeping in the house."

"What about when it gets colder out there?" Diane asked, "We can't expect him to sleep outside when it gets cold."

"We'll get him a kennel or something," Henry said as he scratched behind Shadow's ears. The dog groaned in contentment, "We can fill it with loads of blankets. You could even get the ladies in your knitting circle to make him one. They've been looking for a new project,"

"Maybe," Diane murmured.

She gave one more look out of the window, concern written all over her face, before she turned and walked over to the bed. She sighed as she climbed in between the covers and curled up beside her husband and their dog.

"I don't like him sleeping there," she murmured, "What if the coyotes get him?"

"He's a strong boy," Henry said. "He'll run them off and keep the horses safe I bet."

The couple lapsed into silence and eventually fell asleep.

After that the family fell into a pattern. Every day they would be around each other, going about their daily business. In the evenings they would all sit in the living room, Shadow demanding petting from one owner and Bailey curled up at the feet of the other. Then when it was time for Diane and Henry to go to bed Bailey would trot over to the back door and wait until one of them let him out. Diane would look out of the window, checking that all was well before she got into bed and the couple went to sleep.

Truthfully Bailey liked sleeping outside. He would like it more of course if he could have stayed with Ma and Pop in their bed but he knew that Shadow didn't like it. He could also tell that Ma and Pop got upset every time Shadow and he started fighting. Outside it was nice. The wind smelled lovely and it was always fresh. He could go to the bathroom where ever he liked, whenever he liked and the dishes of water that were left outside for him were always nice and cool on his tongue. Best of all he got to keep his family and their horses safe. He liked the horses, their babies would play with him from time to time and they never minded when he raced around the field that they were eating in.

Once or twice he really kept the family safe. Unknown to Henry and Diane, a coyote showed up on the property, sniffing around and looking for an easy dinner. Even Shadow with his keen eyes and sharp ears hadn't heard the coyote howling. Bailey heard and as soon as he figured out where the sounds were coming from he raced off to chase it away. No one was any the wiser about his night time adventures and Bailey liked it that way.

Of course he didn't always like it outside. When it was raining and thundering he tried to hide under the porch and shelter from the rain. The thunder hurt his ears and the bright flashes of lightening made his eyes burn, leaving his vision spotted and blurred. But he stayed outside because it was better than inside at night. And he loved Diane and Henry and wanted to stay close to them.

Chapter 3

A Walk Across the Road

Bailey liked it at Ma and Pops house. Diane and Henry showed him lots of love at all hours of the day. Still, he felt like something was missing. Being a dog he couldn't understand what, although he thought that it might have something to do with Shadow. He loved Diane and Henry dearly and he liked Shadow a lot but Shadow didn't seem to like him at all. But he still wasn't completely happy.

It was the sleeping outside that got to Bailey the most. He liked it for the most part but sometimes he just wanted to be curled up with Diane and Henry at the bottom of their bed. He wanted cuddles in the night when the thunder hurt his ears and the lightening hurt his eyes. He wanted to have a hand on his head as soon as woke up, to wake Ma and Pop up with a warm lick to the face and laughter. He could do that now and then, when one of them fell asleep during the day but it just wasn't enough for him.

The visitors that the farm got from time to time were nice as well. They would cuddle him and pet him while he sat by their feet. But even with all of that attention he felt he was being left out. It was Shadow that ruled the home, it was Shadow who controlled when they got fed, when they got water and who he could get some cuddles from and when.

One day he was lying out in the sun by the kennel that Henry made for him. It was all quiet on the farm, Ma and Pop went to the local market and took Shadow with them. Bailey was lounging in the sun, watching the little butterflies floating around the meadow. He could hear the horses eating there, the foals frolicking around in the summer sun. They were getting big now and their legs were long and gangly. He couldn't play with them any more even though he wanted to. They didn't know how big they were now and they sometimes stood on his paws.

He was bored. Then some new sounds reached his sharp ears. It was the rumbling of trucks, the clanking of metal together, the thudding of wooden poles together and the hammering of hammers on nails. He had never heard anything like it, not since he left the city. Now he was hearing it again and it wasn't a sound that belonged on The Hill. He stood up and shook his fur out. Flecks of dust and grass flew through the air. After a stretch he trotted off across the grass.

The drive was quiet and covered in dust. There hadn't been any rain for a few days and the ground was turning to dust and the grass around the edges was beginning to turn brown. It was a long walk and by the time he reached the tarmac of the road he was panting heavily. He sat there for a moment, settling his rump in the shade of the tree. Cars drove past now and then, bringing with them a wave of cool air filled with the scent of metal. He could hear the sounds louder now, they were coming from across the road.

Now and then, through the trees, he caught the flash of light on metal and saw a truck drive up the other driveway. There were a few trickles of water running down the driveway to pool on the road. They were too tempting for Bailey to ignore and he was too thirsty to ignore. He trotted quickly across the road, keeping an ear out for cars, and crouched beside the puddle. He lapped at the water, tasting mud and a little bit of cement but most of all it tasted fresh and perfect. His tongue splattered the puddled water across his nose, staining his yellow fur lightly yellow.

He sat in the shade on the other side of the road once more. He panted for breath and to cool down. It was hot by the road, the dark tar seemed to be reflecting the heat and the light right on to him. The noise got even louder before suddenly it stopped. He could hear people talking now, chatting among themselves. Bailey's interest was piqued again and he stood once more. The trip up the drive didn't take as long as he expected, it wasn't quite as long as Ma and Pop's. When he came out into a big bunch of fields he was amazed by what he saw. He had adventures on this side of the road before but it was always a bunch of fields. Something had leveled it all out and there were struts of wood poking out of concrete up into the air. There were a few men dotted around, wearing bright yellow vests and hard orange hats. The light was shining off those too. Scattered around the muddy and torn up ground around the strange building work there were dozens of piles of metal and wood and parked trucks.

***

"I'm telling you Dad," Mark said loudly, "This is going to be a great home for us."

They sat on the hood of their truck, sharing the sandwiches that they'd picked up from the supermarket. The new house was right in front of them, but it was still really basic.

"The foundation took longer than I thought," Ben said quietly, "At this rate we're never going to get the house finished by Christmas."

"We'll get finished Dad," Mark said slowly, "Now the foundation's all finished things will go so much quicker."

"Hey!" Ben said suddenly, "Who's that?"

Mark looked around, searching the building sight for an unknown person. There was no one around that wasn't supposed to be there. Then he realized that his dad was actually looking off towards the drive and followed his gaze. There, sat at the top of the drive, was a little yellow dog. Mark climbed down from the hood and set his lunch to one side. He grabbed a spare bottle of water and slowly made his way towards where the dog sat panting.

"Hello there little guy," he said quietly as he got closer, "Who are you?"

Bailey stepped a little closer, his tail beginning to come up and wag gently.

Mark knelt down and poured a little water into his hand.

"You thirsty guy?" he said, holding out the water filled hand, "Here you go."

Bailey sniffed gently at the hand full of water before quickly lapping it up. His tail wagged harder than before.

When the water was all gone Bailey nuzzled Mark's hand and licked it a little more.

"Well aren't you friendly?!" he said happily, "Where'd you come from?"

Mark rubbed at Bailey's head, scratching just behind the dog's ears the way that he liked. Bailey's tail wagged harder and harder. The dog sat down and leaned against Mark's leg. He noticed a collar around the yellow Labrador's neck and started to shift it around, looking for some form of tags. He found on and saw the address was for the house across the street. More importantly there was a name on it.

"So, Bailey huh?" Mark said. "Is that your name then? Bailey?"

Bailey barked, he was agreeing with what Mark was saying.

"Who's your new friend then?" Ben said as he walked over, "He looks friendly,"

"His name's Bailey," Mark said, "He lives in that farm across the street,"

"He looks very thirsty," Ben said, "Here, put the water in this,"

Mark took the plastic box that Ben was holding out. He placed it on the floor and slowly poured the water. Bailey put his nose in it, lapping up the water before Mark had a chance to finish pouring. Mark stood and watched as Bailey lapped up all the water that he could. Ben stood and watched his son with his new dog friend.

"Come on Mark," Ben said, clapping his son hard on the back, "Time to get back to work. This house isn't going to build itself you know."

The two men turned away and began to walk back towards the building site. Then Mark heard the soft padding of feet and a small bark from behind him. He turned and saw Bailey following them close behind.

"No boy," Mark said. Bailey stopped and looked at him, head tilted to one side, "You need to stay here,"

Bailey continued to walk towards them both. He sat at Mark's feet and started up at him, whining softly. Mark smiled and knelt down, scratching behind Bailey's ears.

"You need to stay here Bailey," he said softly, "If you come too close you might get hurt. We don't want that do we?"

Bailey barked softly and licked Mark's hand.

"That's what I thought," He said, "Now you stay right here and watch. Try to stay out of trouble. I don't want to tell your owners that you got squashed by a digger."

Mark turned and continued to walk away. Bailey sat where he was left and watched the two men and their small crew work. Mark would look over now and then and see him there. Once or twice he spotted his father or one of the other men slipping over with a bowl which they filled with water. He couldn't help but smile when he saw that or when he noticed them giving the dog a gentle pat from time to time.

Having Bailey around seemed to do wonders for the morale of the builders. They seemed to work harder, build faster and stronger and by the end of the day what would normally have taken two days to put together only taken a single day. At some point in the afternoon Bailey left. Mark looked over to the tree where Bailey had been sitting and he was gone. For a moment the man's heart leapt into his throat as he scanned the building site for any flash of yellow fur. He worried that something happened to the yellow dog. That evening he went to the address that he noted on Bailey's license.

The moment he set foot at the end of the driveway, the front door of the house in sight a flash of brown and black burst across the garden, barking and snarling. Mark cried out and backed away quickly. Still this strange brown and black dog continued to come towards him, snarling madly. He started shouting, calling for help from the owners. But the dog was getting closer and closer. Mark felt a tree against his back and quickly turned and leapt for one of the low lying branches. His aim was true and his hands caught hold of the rough bark. He slowly pulled himself into the tree, legs kicking wildly as he pulled himself in.

He crouched there, looking down at the German Shepherd that leapt up at the tree, still barking hard.

"Shadow!" a female voice shouted, "Shadow, leave that boy alone!"

A figure walked across the front yard, her stride brisk and sharp. For a moment the dog climbed away from the tree and looked towards his owner. Then he turned again and continued to watch Mark. The dog growled as Mark lowered a foot down from the branch, preparing to climb from the tree. He quickly pulled his foot back up to the branch.

"Shadow!" the woman shouted again, "Leave him."

The dog walked back a few paces and sat beside the woman's feet as she stood beneath the boughs of the tree.

"Hello," she said, "I'm Diane, what are you doing on my property?"

"My name's Mark," he said, "I'm building a house across the street. I met your dog Bailey earlier today but I didn't see him leave. I wanted to make sure that he's ok."

"You met Bailey?" Diane said surprised, "So that's where he got to,"

"He's ok then?" Mark asked, "It's just I looked up one time and there was no sign of him,"

"He's fine," Dianne said with a smile. "Why don't you come down from that tree and see for yourself?"

Mark climbed down, groaning with relief as his limbs straightened again at last. He reached out and took the hand that Diane offered, even as Shadow growled at him. Diane shooed the angry dog away and led Mark around the back of her house to where Bailey lay in the shade of his kennel, gnawing at a bone that Ma and Pop had brought back for him. He barked when he saw Mark but didn't move.

***

"Hey Mark," Harry, one of the builders shouted, "Looks like your friend's back."

Mark looked up from where he was kneeling on the roof, hammering together some joists. Sure enough, just as Harry said, there sat Bailey in the shade of Mark's car. The yellow dog was panting as usual, his mouth open and tongue hanging out. Bailey looked for all the world like he was smiling with happiness. Mark called to Bailey and the dog looked right at him, his tail wagging. He barked happily and lay down, rolling on to his back and flashing his pale white belly at the builders.

It was fast becoming a usual sight around the building. Every day, rain or shine, Bailey appeared at mid-morning.

He would take his seat beside Mark's truck or inside the front cab if it was raining and he would stay there. The builders loved having him around and would race to see who could finish their particular task and go and play with the dog for a short while. Lunch times too became a time where they all had fun, playing fetch and racing around with Bailey chasing them. The time went faster that way, the building went faster as the builders worked to be the first to finish.

If it was too hot to run around in the sun at midday, as it was from time to time, Bailey would wander over to sit beneath a tree where Mark would join him. They would share a drink and Mark would slip Bailey a few treats he took to carrying around with him. The two would sit quietly beside each other, passing the time when they took a break.

"Mark!" Ben shouted, breaking Mark's concentration, "Ben we've got a problem!"

"What?" Mark called back, "It better not be another late delivery."

"No son!" Ben said, "But one of our bags has gone missing,"

"Bags of what?" Mark asked, sticking his head over the edge of the roof.

"Cement," Ben said, looking up, "One of our bags of cement has gone missing."

"What would someone do with a single bag of cement?" Mark asked.

"I don't know," Ben said with a shrug, "But it's gone,"

"Maybe someone's building a very small pond?" Harry suggested.

Mark gave him a withering look and began to climb down from the roof. His boots thudded heavily on the metal rungs. When he hit the ground the builders were all gathered around talking about the missing cement bag. He glanced towards his truck out of habit but saw no sign of Bailey.

"Hey, where's Bailey?" he asked everyone.

The builders looked around and shrugged.

"Maybe the cement thief stole the dog too," Harry said with a laugh.

"Not funny," Mark snapped, "Diane and Henry are going to be so upset if something's happened to Bailey."

"I don't think that's going to be a problem," Ben said.

His arms were crossed over his chest and he was staring over towards the side of the building. Mark followed his gaze and couldn't help but laugh. It seemed that not only did his father find the missing bag of cement but he also found the missing dog. The first part of Bailey that they spotted was his wagging tail. His rear end was bouncing back and forth as he tugged and pulled at something behind the wall. The sound of something plastic and heavy being dragged across the ground came to them then. Bailey moved further and further out into the open until eventually Mark saw the flash of something white clamped between the dog's teeth. Bailey continued to tug on the bag of cement, drawing it further and further out as he bounced up and down on his legs.

"Bailey!" Mark shouted, "Drop it!"

Bailey let the bag go and sat down, looking at Mark with pride for what he accomplished. Mark walked over and hefted the bag of cement onto his shoulder. He was surprised to see that there wasn't a mark on the plastic of the bag at all.

"Naughty boy," Mark said, pointing at Bailey, "You're a very naughty dog."

Bailey whined softly and lay down. He rested his head on his front paws and looked up at Mark. Mark couldn't help himself. He laughed and tossed the bag to someone else before he knelt down in front of the dog and ruffled the fur on the top of his head.

"You have got to stop stealing things," he said gently, "Really, it can't go on."

It wasn't the first time that Bailey stole something from the building site. It was often the case in fact that whenever a tool went missing the first place that the builders looked would be wherever Bailey was. Some of the things that the yellow dog managed to carry away were amusing, once or twice he even managed to drag an entire wheelbarrow from one side of the site to the other. Bailey's thefts became so common that the builders would place bets on what he would steal next. Mark managed to make a small fortune in bets from that. Life on the building site was never as boring or as dull as it was before Bailey arrived on the scene.

***

"Look at it son," Ben said, "Look at what we've built."

Ben and Mark stood side by side. They looked up at the house that they built. Bailey sat by Mark's feet, inspecting the building himself. When Mark opened the front door Bailey raced ahead of him and shoved his way through the small gap. The dog disappeared into the darkness of the house as the two men shouted after him.

"I guess he likes it," Mark said eventually when Bailey didn't return.

Bailey liked it so much in fact that when all of Ben and Mark's belongings were placed in their new home he didn't leave. He disappeared for a few hours but returned just before dark and within moments of being let in Bailey was fast asleep at the foot of Mark's bed. The man had no choice but to climb in and lay around the dog. Sometime in the night Bailey crawled up to lay beside him and when he awoke the next morning Mark's arm was around him, playing with his soft floppy ears. Bailey felt as he was home at last.

He liked living with Ben and Mark. They were always there to play with him and he always got to sleep on one of the beds with them. Mark tried to return him to Ma and Pop's once or twice but come sunset Bailey always managed to find his way back to the other house and was barking at the door to be let in.

"I'm sorry Diane," Mark said one day as Diane walked over the road to see where Bailey was, "I've tried to bring him back to you but he always comes back,"

"I don't blame him," Diane said, stroking Bailey's head. "Shadow hasn't exactly made it easy for him to live with us,"

"Hmmm," Mark hummed in agreement. He remembered the mean Shepherd all too well, "I can't blame him for that then."

"It may be better if we just say that he lives with you now," Diane said with a shrug, "I mean you're around a lot and he gets lots more attention than he ever could with us. It might be better for him to live with a family with no other dog,"

"I do like having him around," Mark said, rubbing Bailey's side, "He likes to come with us on the builds. The crew loves him too,"

"Well isn't that good?!" Diane said, "He seems to have found where he belongs at last,"

"Are you sure your daughter won't mind?" Mark asked, "I know she asked you to look after him for her and her friend. Don't they want him back?"

"No, I'm afraid not," Diane said sadly. "Amanda's practice has gotten busier and busier and now Janie's got her own family. They couldn't take him back even if they wanted to."

"Well I guess that's it then," Mark said, "Bailey's our dog now. You can come to visit him of course. Lord knows Dad likes the company from time to time,"

"Oh you can be sure of it." Diane said with a laugh.

***

And so it was that Bailey now lived with Mark and Ben. Now and then the yellow dog would travel across the road to see his old owners. They always welcomed him with a nice bowl of water and some scratching behind his ears but he rarely stayed long. Shadow seemed to like this new living arrangement much better than the old one. He no longer snarled at Bailey or tried to chase him away. In fact the other dog left him alone completely, acting like he weren't there. For Bailey this was wonderful but he felt a little sad when he realized that if he tried to go back to living with Henry and Diane things would go back to the way that they were before.

He was content to live with Mark. Mark took him for long walks and gave him real pieces of meat for dinner from time to time, not just canned dog food. He took Bailey in his truck to other building sites and he was allowed to play games with the builders. Each night he slept beside his new master and each morning he got to wake up beside him as well. Bailey liked to wake Mark up by licking his face. It made Mark laugh and play with him right away. Sometimes he was a little grumpy and usually would just let Bailey out of the room and then go back to bed.

Time passed and although Bailey didn't realize it, it would soon be a year he began living with Ben and Mark. Things continued as usual and he was happy. Then one day Ben and Mark loaded up the truck like they always did but when Bailey jumped into the cab Mark lifted him out again and put him on the deck. Bailey went to follow Mark back to the truck but Mark ordered him to stay. Bailey didn't want to make Mark sad, or worse angry, so he was a good dog and stayed where he was.

He watched the truck drive off with his humans inside and lay down in the sun. At first it was nice, just like when he first moved to the Hill. But then the time continued to pass and his humans still weren't back. They left him food and water which was just strange. Normally they left him water, but never food. He went across the road to Ma and Pop's house but they weren't there either. He decided to go and play with the horses in the fields. There were new foals Bailey liked to race around with and it gave him something to do.

The sun was beginning to set by the time Bailey made it back to the deck and he was starving. There was no sign of the truck so Bailey decided to eat the food that was left out. It was dark out by the time he ate so he lay down on the hard wooden deck and went to sleep. Eventually his keen ears caught the sound of slamming doors and he smelled his humans had returned.

He scrambled to his feet and raced around the house. He barked and wagged his tail, making sure that they both knew how happy he was to have them back. Mark smiled and ruffled his fur but didn't do much more than that. Ben just trudged past the happy yellow dog and let himself into the house. Mark followed his father and Bailey watched him. He whined gently, confused. Today was a very strange day.

"I'm sorry boy," Mark said with a sigh, "It's been a long day. We're both really tired."

Bailey followed Mark into the house and just watched his master go about his duties. He stayed to one side, making sure that he didn't get in the way. When Mark got into bed that night Bailey was a little nervous about climbing up beside him.

"Come on!" Mark said, patting the blankets beside him, "Come on up."

Bailey's tail wagged and he jumped up on to the bed. He quickly lay down beside Mark and welcomed the tummy rub that the human gave him. Maybe things weren't too different after all.

"I'm sorry you were alone all day today," Mark murmured quietly, "We've got a job in the city and it's going to take us a lot longer than we thought it would to get done."

Bailey barked softly, he didn't understand exactly what Mark meant but he knew that being away from him bothered Mark.

"And it's going to keep happening I'm afraid," Mark said, "You're going to have a lot more days alone. We'll make sure that you have lots of water and food for you but we can't be here to let you in and out of the house. We won't tie you up, just leave you on the deck. Diane and Henry are bringing your old kennel over so you've got somewhere to sleep if it rains. That'll be nice won't it?"

Bailey barked happily again. Mark continued to stroke him but said no more. Eventually the gentle movements of the human's fingers faded away and he started to softly snore.

***

Ben and Mark were indeed away a lot more often. After a while they weren't as tired when they got home so they were able to play with Bailey like they used to. But it was still boring during the day. Bailey had no one to play with, no one to give him cuddles or talk to him. It was boring on the deck, only the bees were around to keep him company. Then Bailey realized that he wasn't tied up. And then he remembered the new people that he found on his last adventure. In fact his last adventure gave him a lovely new family. Maybe it was time to have another adventure.

With his mind made up Bailey climbed to his feet and gave himself a shake. He trotted down the steps of the deck and disappeared into the woods around the house. His secret walks began.

Chapter 4

Old Man Joe

At first Bailey stayed close to his new home on his new adventures. He explored the surrounding woods and fields. He walked along the quiet paths of the forest, chased the deer and the butterflies. He soon knew every part of the woods around him and even when the fog of winter came down from the mountains and made it difficult to see any more than three tree trunks away Bailey still knew the way.

He enjoyed his adventures through the woods but still he wanted something more. He visited Ma and Pop from time to time, playing with the horses and Shadow when he was in a good mood. Sometimes he even stayed the night, curled up in front of a warm fire, dry from the rain. On the warm dry nights Bailey took to staying in the forest, finding a nice cave in the side of a hill to sleep in or the hollowed out trunk of a long dead tree. It was nice out there in the woods, cool and quiet and he found a peace among the trees that was so missing in the world of his humans.

As time passed Bailey continued to explore the forests and explored more and more of The Hill. There were a few houses around, spread out wide with vast fields and woods in between them. The roads were quiet, little more than dirt paths and he rarely worried about any cars coming along to hurt him. He usually heard them coming over the quiet of the birds singing. He never went close to the houses, he decided that the humans inside seemed happy enough and he didn't want to disturb them. But he would sit among the trees and watch them going about their lives.

One day he was racing through the trees, chasing a rabbit he managed to sniff out, when his collar caught on a branch, the wood slipping easily through a gap between the leather and his furred back. Bailey didn't know this of course, all he knew was that one moment he was running along, the white tail of the rabbit bouncing up and down just in front of him, and the next he was dragged to a halt and bouncing backwards. Whatever was stopping him from running was attached to something at his neck. It reminded him of when Janie and Amanda took him out among the streets of the big cities and attached a long line to his neck. It stopped him from running after the bright yellow cars and yanked him sharply back just like what was happening now. Bailey wasn't able to see for himself what was holding him back, he couldn't bend his head far enough. He wiggled and shook as hard as he could, yanking and tugging.

Whatever was holding him in place was strong but flexible. It twisted and moved with him and pulled him around as well. Every time that he pulled one way and thought that he was free he would relax and be dragged back to where he started. Eventually though, as he continued to pull he heard a snapping sound, like a branch breaking but somehow different. Bailey was still pulling against the hold and when it broke he stumbled and fell over his paws to fall on the ground.

Quickly Bailey climbed to his feet and looked back. A strip of leather was hanging from the branch. He remembered seeing it once before, in Amanda's hands before she brought him out here to The Hill. It had been tighter then, when she had put it around his neck. The leather had felt strange around his neck when it was first put there, constricting but somehow comforting. It had been stiff to move too, hard to twist and rigid against his flesh. Over time it grew softer and Bailey forgot it was there. He couldn't understand why it was now here, in the woods with him, hanging from a branch. His neck felt strange now too, lighter somehow and whenever he moved there was no sound of metal tapping gently together. The yellow dog never realized that it was him making the noise, he thought it was just a sound that was always in the air.

Bailey bounced around, enjoying that the sound was no longer there. Then he heard it again and saw the leather strap bouncing with the branch as the wind blew. The wind was cold on the bare strip of skin around his neck where the strap rubbed the fur away. Bailey barked and raced away, trying to escape that sound. Eventually, when he ran far enough the sound was completely gone. Bailey looked back over his shoulders as he raced away and the sound faded. Then he stumbled and fell again, tripping over his paws. He rolled over and over, down a small hill in the woods to land in a dusty pile on the dry earth at the bottom. His yellow fur was no longer bright and shining. Instead it was now a dull brown color, patchy and dark.

Bailey was a little sore from the fall but quickly climbed to his feet again and ran back into the woods. Every move that he made sent plumes of dust flying from his coat into the air. He was not too far from home, he knew that although he wasn't quite sure where he was, the fall having thrown his mind a little. He knew he was lost but he had a vague idea of where to go and he was sure that sooner or later his nose would guide him in the right direction. Bailey shook himself, sending the dust from his fall flying into the air around him in a massive cloud. His coat wasn't quite yellow once more but he wasn't far off. He sniffed the air and headed in a direction that smelled more familiar to him than any other way.

***

Everyone called him Old Man Joe, even he called himself that. The people on The Hill left him alone and he left them alone. He lived far in the woods, in a small shack with no electricity and no water. There were a few meadows nearby and some flower gardens that sparkled brightly with color so Old Man Joe kept bees. They were his sole source of income, giving him honey to sell at the farmer's market and allowing him to buy the few essentials that he couldn't provide for himself. He even had an arrangement with some of the local farmers, trading honey for milk and meat rather than having to go into town himself to get it. Many on The Hill thought that Joe was crazy, either because he wanted to live alone so far away from everything or because he kept to himself as much as he could.

Joe was a simple man who just wanted the simple life. He wanted no one to rely on him and he didn't want to rely on anyone else if he could help it. So he lived alone, provided for himself and he liked it that way. He had his shack, the woods around him and the bees and he was almost completely self-sufficient. When times were hard or the weather was particularly terrible, especially in winter, one or two of the nearby neighbors, the ones who weren't afraid to go near him that is, would call in from time to time. They would bring spare blankets or firewood that they didn't need and check that he was ok. Other times they would come to buy some of his honey. Many claimed that it was more delicious than anything else that they ever tasted.

It was to Old Man Joe's shack that Bailey's adventures first took him. Joe was in the process of building himself a new house, a bigger warmer cabin than the one that he had now. The shack was nice enough, it was still sturdy and able to stand up to even the worst weather. Joe was getting older and the winter that just past left him cold and shivering in his shack, even under the layers of blankets and furs that he wrapped himself in. His joints still ached from time to time and the draft from the door frames, warped with age still plagued his memory. So Joe decided to build a new cabin, of thick logs and moss to plug the gaps. He went so far as to trade many, many jars of honey for some expertly made windows of thick glass to keep out the wind.

Just like Ben and Mark, Joe was eating his lunch when he first caught sight of Bailey. The first sign that something was coming came from Bear. Bear was a big brown dog of indiscriminate breed that was with Joe since he was a puppy. He kept Joe safe and gave him the company he needed to ensure that he wouldn't go mad out in the woods alone. Joe was eating his lunch, Bear resting by his feet when the dog suddenly looked up and stared off towards the woods. Joe looked up and followed Bear's gaze but saw nothing. He knew that there was something out there, Bear never was wrong. Joe rested a hand on Bear's big brown head and patted him gently.

Then he saw it, a flash of brownish yellow that was bright among the browns and greens of the forest. Slowly he lowered the sandwich and picked up a stick that leaned against the log that he sat on. Joe's gaze was locked upon the woods and the movement that was still happening among the leaves. Then Bear barked and the leaves burst open. A round of barking came from a dog that wasn't Bear and something came rushing towards the dog and the man Joe shot to his feet, ignoring the pains in his joints, and raised his stick above his head with a yell. He waved it around, shouting and hollering. The thing just kept coming towards them.

Joe paused as the creature stopped moving and stared at him. Bear wasn't growling, instead he stood up, barking and wagging his tail wildly. The creature was another dog, a yellow Labrador covered in dirt and dust. Joe lowered his stick and put it back against the log. Bear walked over to the new dog and they engaged in a sniffing greeting while Joe sat down and returned to eating his sandwich. He watched the two dogs as they started to jump around each other, playing and barking with happiness.

He smiled as he saw the way that Bear's tail was wagging, he couldn't remember seeing the dog so happy in a while. He felt a little bit of guilt within himself for keeping other people and other dogs away from Bear, a dog that so clearly enjoyed the company of other animals. But there was a friend for him now, here just as Joe was trying to think of a way to keep his dog out of the way while he was building his new cabin. Bear groaned and slumped on the ground. The dog stretched out his legs and sprawled across the ground, tongue hanging out and tail still wagging. He was clearly exhausted from playing with his new friend.

The new dog wasn't tired, at least not yet, and he walked up to Joe. Joe watched the dog come closer and eventually held a hand out towards it. The dog didn't even flinch at the sudden movement. Instead it shoved its head into the man's hand and wagged its tail.

"Well hey there Buddy," Joe said quietly, scratching the dog's ear.

The dog's tail wagged even harder and it barked softly at the words.

"Oh you like that do you?" Joe said, scratching harder, "Is it the name or the scratch you like more I wonder?"

The dog let him scratch a little more before moving to lay beside Bear in the shade of some logs. Joe smiled and stood with a groan, deciding that it was time to go back to work. For the rest of the day the two dogs played together and watched Joe work at building his new home. At one point the dogs disappeared down into the forest for a few hours. They didn't go far, Joe could hear them barking in the nearby trees and they eventually emerged from the shadows as the day began to cool. They were now both covered in dust and bits of grass and leaves. Joe laughed at the pair of them as they sat side by side, their tongues hanging out of the side of their mouths. Suddenly the new dog barked, turned and disappeared back into the woods. Bear seemed about to follow after it but stopped at the edge of the trees, barked a few times before turning around and returning to Joe's side.

***

The visits from Buddy, as Joe came to call the yellow dog, continued for much of the time that he was building. At first Joe couldn't care more or less whether the dog arrived each day or not but he knew that Bear adored his new friend. On the few days where Buddy didn't appear Bear would mope about Joe's paddock, getting under his feet and generally seeming miserable. Of course the next day Buddy would always appear and be met with lots of bouncing and barking from Bear. Joe truly enjoyed seeing his dog so happy and started to take to Buddy just as Bear did.

Now and then, when Bear was feeling particularly tired from their play he would rest in the shade, leaving Buddy to amuse himself. That was when Buddy and Joe bonded. Normally Buddy would just sit at the edge of the building site that Joe created and watch the man go about his construction. Once or twice he would help in his own way. One day, when trying to use some ropes to hoist a log up to the right height to be lowered into place, Joe's hands slipped and let go of one of the ropes. He cried out, expecting the log to come crashing down and ruin all of his hard work. But it didn't. Joe looked around, trying to figure out what was happening. Buddy grabbed the rope between his jaws, dug in his paws and was holding it in place.

Joe stared for a few moments before the yellow dog, currently clean of dirt for now, whined softly. Then the man rushed forward and took the rope from Buddy's mouth, holding the other ropes tightly. Joe smiled and when the building was done for the day and he was stocking his fire ready for supper he fished out a bit of bacon that he was saving for a special occasion. He fried the bacon and split it between the two dogs, giving Buddy the lion's share as thanks.

Buddy continued to visit, even as the weather began to turn towards autumn and winter. As Joe started to put the finishing touches to his house, specifically hammering on the roof tiles, Buddy and Bear would vanish into the woods for hours. They began to go further afield, so far away that even up on the roof Joe couldn't hear their barks of joy any longer. But Joe never worried. They always returned before it got dark. As it began to rain more often they would come back muddy, wet and covered in twigs and leaves. There was no doubt that the two were happy, the two best friends that Joe had ever seen. He never saw a friendship between two individuals that was so strong, be it human or animal. Joe liked having Buddy there too, not just because Buddy helped him build sometimes but also because he made the one creature that Joe loved more than anything happy.

Joe vaguely wondered from time to time where Buddy went at night, when the yellow dog raced off into the woods. He always seemed well fed and well groomed. He was affectionate and friendly and had no problem with either people or dogs. Sometimes Buddy would stay the night, curled up outside with Bear when it was still warm enough to do so. Most of the time Buddy would head off to wherever he lived and return again the next morning. There was no doubt in Joe's mind that Buddy had a family somewhere on

The Hill that loved him and looked after him. And then he found himself wondering if they knew about the little dog's adventures.

***

One day Buddy and Bear were out in the woods, exploring as they usually did when Buddy realized that there was a strange smell in the air. It was different from anything that he ever smelled before, musky and meaty. It reminded him a little of other dogs but there was something different about it. He didn't know what it was but for some reason the new smell made the fur on the back of his neck rise up and he wanted to growl. Bear smelled the ground along with him and stared at him. The brown dog didn't know what the strange smell was either. Together they decided to follow it, Buddy taking the lead because his nose was better.

Meanwhile Joe was on top of his roof, nailing in a few more roof tiles before he took a break for lunch. He stood, one leg over either side of the top beam and looked out over the fields around him. The colorful heads of autumn flowers were bobbing up and down in the breeze. He could see his bees flitting around between the flowers and buzzing away back to their hives, laden down with pollen. Everything else was silent, there were no birds singing in the trees or the rustling of leaves made by deer or rabbits. He looked around and saw something big moving out of the woods close to the hives.

There were a pair of binoculars attached to his belt and Joe reached for them, unclipping them and bringing them up to his eyes. He looked through the lenses, twisted a knob to focus the sights and gasped. It was a bear! A brown bear from the looks of it and well fed. It was probably getting ready for its winter hibernation and his bees and honey were in his sights.

He started shouting, waved his arms in the air in an attempt to get the bear away from his hives before it had a chance to ruin them. The bear simply turned to look at him before continuing to lumber its way towards the hives. Joe's heart pounded. If the bear got into the hives and ate all of the honey he would be left without any source of income. The bees were already beginning to slow down their production, getting ready to go into hibernation until the flowers came out again in the spring. The hives had one last harvest in them before Joe left the honey that remained to see the bees through winter. The bear would eat it all and his bees would probably die of starvation before spring came.

Then something moved in the trees, in the same place where the bear came from. It was two creatures, both smaller than the bear, one brown and one yellow. For a second Joe thought that the shapes were cubs, oddly colored but following their mother. Then he turned the binoculars on them and saw that it was in fact Buddy and Bear. He shouted, trying to get the two dogs away from the bear before it could notice them. It would likely kill them if they got too close. His grandfather drilled into him never to come between a bear and its food.

Bear stopped and looked at his master. The brown dog trotted towards the cabin. Buddy stopped too for a moment and looked up at Joe. Joe shouted, calling the yellow dog and trying to get him to return. But Buddy didn't hear him, or more likely simply ignored the human which was more likely. The dog continued to run towards the bear, barking now and growling.

Buddy didn't like this strange smelling thing that was heading towards his new friend's bees. He liked his new friend and he liked the bees that flew around. Their little feet tickled his nose when they landed on it and made him sneeze. He knew that the bees were important to the old man, that they helped him have bacon to give to him and Bear and that he spent a lot of time just sitting among the hives as the bees flew around him. And now the strange big creature was going to hurt the bees, maybe even eat the sticky sweet smelling goo that came out of their homes sometimes.

He barked and snarled, getting closer to the thing. It got bigger and bigger the closer that he got and then it reared up, standing on two legs like a person. It wasn't a person. It was big, with claws and a thick coat of brown hair that was so like his best friend Bear's fur. He skidded to a halt in front of the creature, his claws digging into the ground and sending up little clouds of dust. He barked, lowered his head towards the ground and snarled. The creature fell to its front legs and sniffed at him. It made a strange growling sound that was part dog and part cow, or at least it seemed that way to Buddy. It swung a massive paw at him but Buddy was too fast and leapt backwards, out of the way.

Buddy bounced and nipped at the creature's flanks, being careful not to actually break the skin. He had a lot of practice at that when he helped Ben and Mark moved those heavy bags of grey dust around when they were building their house. The creature tried to chase him, tried to swat at him with its massive claws but it was too slow and Buddy was too agile and quick. The creature began to move away from the bees' home, back towards the forest and Buddy kept chasing it.

Joe watched in awe as Buddy chased the bear, darting in and out, barking and biting. The bear apparently wasn't angry at this, it just seemed to be making worried noises that he heard a time or two when out hunting. It sniffed and growled softly but every time it tried to hit out at Buddy it missed. Slowly Buddy was backing it away towards the woods. Joe's jaw dropped open as the bear turned and ran off into the woods again, moving quickly for so large a beast.

He climbed down from the roof and rushed over to his field. Buddy stood in the meadow, barking after the bear. The yellow dog turned to look at Joe and his tongue lolled from his mouth. His tail wagged merrily; he saw it as all a game. Joe rushed forwards and knelt beside the dog, wrapping his strong arms around the canine and ruffling his fur.

"Who's a good boy," Joe crooned in the dog's ear, "Who's a good boy who chased off the big nasty bear?"

Bear barked at hearing his name and butted against his master. Joe reached up and rubbed one of Bear's ears as well.

"Not you, you big fool," he said, laughing, "Your Buddy here saved my bees. I think he deserves a place with us now, don't you?"

***

After that Joe found a new warmth in his heart for Buddy. Once his cabin was finished he moved Bear's dog house over to sit outside his front door. Then he built one for Buddy too, right next to Bear's house. He wanted Buddy to know that there was always a place for him with Joe and Bear. Buddy seemed to take it as such, coming around and sometimes staying a few more nights than he did before. Joe started to make sure to always have bacon in his cooler.

Every morning he would cook it and within moments of taking it off the small stove that he cooked it on Buddy would appear from the woods and race towards the house. Joe made sure to leave the door propped open enough to let the two dogs squeeze through and he always found himself smiling whenever he heard the clicking of dog nails on the wooden slats of his porch.

Buddy was happy. He had a new family to live with and there was always food waiting for him when he turned up. He wanted to have another adventure and see who else he could make friends with.

Chapter 5

Charlie and Bob

It was a long winter and Bailey spent most of it inside Ben and Mark's house. As the weather turned colder and snow began to cover the ground the two men began to keep Bailey inside, worried that leaving him outside would leave him too cold, possibly even frozen to death. At least that's what Mark said as he kept Bailey inside in the mornings. Bailey liked being warm certainly, but he liked running through the snow more and when Ben let him out in the evenings when both men returned from their work in the city he was the happiest he had ever been.

What Bailey missed the most during those dark, cold, winter months was the adventures that he would take. He missed visiting Ma and Pop, he missed spending time with Old Man Joe and playing through the woods with Bear. He wanted to meet as many new people as he could and new dogs too but staying inside meant that he couldn't.

Finally the weather began to warm slightly although snow still covered the ground. Mark and Ben took the time to fit a doggy door to their back door, realizing that they needed to let Bailey come and go as he pleased. And now, with the weather warming it was no longer too cold to walk far on the ground, Bailey was looking forward to taking a new adventure and seeing what new people he could meet. As he listened to Ben and Mark driving away in their clunking truck he stood at the window and looked out.

Once they were out of sight Bailey bounded through the house and out of the dog door, leaving it swinging and creaking in his wake. He leapt down from the deck and landed in a pile of snow, sending it flying into the air around him. The sun was bright and the sky blue but Bailey's breath still came out of his mouth in a cloud. Bailey threw his nose in the air and breathed in deeply, catching a distant, faint scent that reminded him of where he should go first.

It was faint, almost too faint to pick up but Bailey had a strong nose and he knew the smell well. It was a scent that spoke to him and reminded him a favorite part of his adventures. It was bacon and he knew exactly where to go to find it. So Bailey set off through the forest, leaping over the now bare trees and bushes. Birds tweeted and a few rabbits and squirrels were bouncing around.

Bailey raced through the forest, following the unmarked path that he knew so well. Within a few minutes he burst out of the tree line and saw ahead of him Joe's well built little cabin. A candle burned in the window and the door was slightly propped open, a narrow gap just big enough to let a dog of Bailey's size through. The chimney smoked and the smell of bacon surrounded the cabin and Joe's little garden. Bailey barked and raced up the stairs where he was immediately met by the barking form of his best friend Bear. Joe smiled when he saw the cause of the commotion.

"Well it's good to see you Buddy," he said happily. He stepped back and held the door open, "Come on in fellah."

***

It was a few hours before Bailey left Joe's house, having munched down a hearty breakfast of bacon and bread. Joe and Bear were really glad to see him but after being cooped up all winter he wanted to explore and hopefully meet a new person or two at last. He bid his friend farewell and allowed Joe one last scratch behind the ears before he burst out of the door and into the snow once more. Softly Bailey padded through the snow and out towards the road. It was as quiet as usual, the snow that covered the gravel and dirt barely touched and still firm. He bounded across the road and up a drive on the other side.

He had seen the drive before, on his adventures with Bear, but he had never been up it. Joe had mentioned the names of the people who lived there, Charlie and Bob. From what Bailey understood they were two men who lived together and loved each other. Joe didn't seem to like that and according to the old man neither did many who lived on The Hill. But then again Bailey knew that Joe didn't really like many people so what did Joe know. Bailey decided that as long as they were friendly he didn't care. The only thing that he cared about was making new friends.

The drive, just like all of the other drives Bailey found, was long and winding. There were no tracks on the ground and Bailey couldn't smell anything that was remotely human on the track. But he could smell something, slowly making its way down from the house further up that Bailey could just make out. And he could see a small shape darting around on the square of snow in front of the house. There were two people there as well, stood right next to the house.

Bailey slowly trotted closer. He knew that rushing right up was not a good idea. He'd done it once or twice when he first met Ben and Mark, and Joe and Bear. That didn't go too well. And the small shape that was running around smelled like dog. If he was going to make a new friend Bailey knew that he needed to move slowly so that he didn't scare the little shape. So he made his way further up the driveway, slowly and steadily, not hidden within the bushes.

***

"She's so happy!" Bob said, smiling and wrapping his arm around Charlie's shoulders, "I told you that this was a good idea. She needs to run around outside for a change,"

"But I'm coooold," Charlie complained, snuggling closer to his boyfriend's body, "Can't we just leave her out here and sit inside? The big window can let us watch her."

"You know that's a bad idea," Bob said with a sigh, "If something happens to her we can't get to her quickly if we're inside. Besides, you need some fresh air too,"

Charlie didn't say anything. He sulked and stuck out his tongue at Bob. Bob chuckled and leaned forward to kiss him on the cheek.

"Yes Mom," Charlie said sarcastically.

He settled back against Bob's chest and watched as their little gray dog raced around the garden. She was churning up the snow, revealing the green grass beneath. She trotted back and forth across the garden, nose lowered to the snow and her tail wagging wildly. Now and then she would leap in the air and pound down onto the ground. She would bark and yap before racing around as though something was chasing her.

"Well at least Lulu's having fun," Charlie muttered.

He shivered and rubbed his arms to warm them up. Bob chuckled and suddenly wrapped his arms around Charlie, a thick blanket held tightly in his arms. Charlie sighed and leaned his head back on Bob's shoulder as he was surrounded by warmth at last. The two men stood there and watched Lulu racing around the garden. Suddenly she stopped completely and looked towards their drive. Her tail stopped wagging and she stood stock still. Charlie and Bob stiffened and followed the direction of her gaze.

"Is that a dog?" Charlie asked after a moment.

"I think so," Bob said quietly.

A yellow dog stood on their driveway, its fur bright and vibrant against the almost blindingly white snow that was all around. They watched, holding their breath as the yellow dog slowly walked closer. Lulu didn't make a sound or move at all. The yellow dog just kept moving forwards, step by step. It woofed softly and Lulu walked slowly towards it. Charlie gasped as the yellow dog slowly lay on the ground, its tail wagging softly, drawing lines in the snow with its fur. Lulu continued to walk forwards, hesitant and her body shaking slightly. Charlie made to go to her but Bob held him back, gripping tightly to his upper arms.

"Let's see what happens," he whispered quietly into Charlie's ear, "He doesn't seem to want to hurt her."

Charlie watched, his muscles tense, as Lulu walked closer and closer to the yellow dog. Her nose twitched as she got close enough. Then she barked, yipping, and started to bounce around. The yellow dog's rear went up, its tail wagging hard and its tongue hanging out of its open mouth. Then suddenly, without warning the two dogs took off, racing around the yard, taking it in turns to chase each other.

"Well would you look at that," Bob said quietly, "Looks like our little girl's made a new friend."

They held each other and watched, laughing at the antics of the two canines as they enjoyed the snow and fresh air.

***

It was well into spring and the weather was finally beginning to warm up. Bailey was spending more and more time with Charlie and Bob and little Lulu. He was growing to love them more each and every day. They always welcomed him with open arms and Lulu was able to run with him and adventure. Bear was getting older and he couldn't explore the forest as much as the year before. Bailey still liked to visit Bear and Joe and spend time relaxing with them in the sun. But playing through the trees with Lulu was almost as much fun.

"Looks like Sunshine's back," Bob said one spring morning, nudging Charlie with his elbow.

And indeed he was. Lulu was lounging on the grass in the shade of a small bush but as soon as Bailey appeared from between the trees she leapt to her feet and raced over to the other dog. She ran around him in circles, barking happily. The dogs bounced around, chasing each other and barking loudly. Charlie and Bob barked and laughed with enjoyment at seeing their dog and her friend having so much fun.

"I'll go and get them some water," Charlie said, standing up,

"Don't forget the treats," Bob called over his shoulder as Charlie entered the house, "Sunshine, Lulu, time for a little break."

The two dogs barked and turned to race towards the house. They settled down quickly on the deck, lapping at the bowls of water that Charlie put down for them. Then they munched down the chew bones that he brought them too. Satisfied and now tired with their full bellies the dogs lay side by side and settled into a doze.

That was what Bailey liked so much about Charlie and Bob too. There was always something for him to eat and it was almost always tasty and delicious. He adored going to Joe's and having his bacon breakfast but he enjoyed the treats just as much. And when he was there he seemed to have a different name. Just like Ma and Pop and Ben and Mark called him Bailey and Joe called him Buddy, here Bob and Charlie called him Sunshine. He liked that name, just as he liked all of the other names that he was called by. He listened to the two humans when they were discussing what to call him. He liked listening to them, they seemed so in love with each other and Lulu was so special to them. He liked how much they loved her too.

"We don't know who he belongs to," Charlie said one day, "We can't keep him,"

"I'm sure he lives somewhere," Bob said, "He's well looked after, you can see that. And he's obviously not starving."

"But why doesn't he stay there?" Charlie asked, "I mean, if he has a home where he's loved why does he always appear here pretty much everyday?"

"I don't know," Bob said with a sigh, "I guess we'd know more if we actually talked to the people on The Hill and down in town,"

"They won't talk to us," Charlie said harshly, "It's not our fault if we can't find out where he comes from. They won't talk to us just because we love each other so we can't be blamed,"

"We can't just claim him as ours Charlie," Bob said tiredly. It was an argument that they had many times before, "We just have to accept that they don't like us. Things won't change overnight and they're pretty isolated out here."

"I know, I know," Charlie said gently, "I just wish things were a little easier."

They lapsed into silence for a little while, just enjoying each other's company and watching the dogs having fun in the sunshine.

"What should we call him?" Charlie asked after a few minutes, "We can't just call him "Him" all the time,"

"Buttercup?" Bob suggested.

"He's a dog, not a cow," Charlie said. "What about Marigold?"

"He's a he," Bob pointed out, "Sunshine?"

"He is the color of sunshine," Charlie said, looking up into the sky where the sun shone, "And he has brightened up Lulu's life like the sun,"

"Sunshine it is then," Bob said firmly. "I can't believe how much she's changed since he's been around."

It was true. Everyone knew it, even Sunshine/Bailey. Before, Lulu was a trembling mess, jumping at every sound and so nervous about everything she saw. The two men didn't dare leave her on her own in their garden, in case she saw something and panicked, running off into the forest. Now though she was braver and more confident all of the time. She knew that Sunshine would always keep her safe and protect her from anything that might hurt her. With that thought in her doggy mind Lulu was no longer afraid to actually explore. She didn't jump at the slightest sound and she didn't tremble with constant fear. As she got used to the strange sounds of her garden and her humans she began to worry less, even when Sunshine wasn't around. It felt to Bob and Charlie that she was like a completely different dog and for that they loved Sunshine even more.

***

It was getting warmer and warmer on the Hill. Every day dawned bright and clear and it was sunny and hot. It rained now and then but most of the rain came during the night and was soaked into the ground by the next morning. The rain was a good thing, in everyone's eyes. It stopped it from getting too hot and made sure that all the plants everywhere got plenty of water to drink. But for Bailey, Bear and Lulu it was torture. And Shadow became much more ill-tempered because of the heat. Bailey would always go on his adventures with Bear in the morning, before their bacon breakfast, when the day was still cool and Bear still had the energy he needed to run and bounce through the trees.

Then he would go to Lulu's house and they would lie in the garden until it got too hot for both of them. The garden was covered in shade from the trees until midday when the sun was above the tops of the trees. Then it got too hot for them to keep running around. They would lie on the deck behind Bob and Charlie's house, under the little bit of shade that remained, panting for breath and trying to stay cool.

"We need to find a better way to keep them cool," Bob said one day as he and Charlie enjoyed the sun, "They can't get cool enough there, it's too closed in,"

"Well what should we do then?" Charlie asked, fanning himself with a rolled up newspaper,"

"I don't know," Bob said with a shrug. Then he sighed and climbed to his feet, "But I'm going to water the plants, they look a bit thirsty themselves."

It was while Bob was watering the plants that he realized how they could help the two dogs stay cool in the ever increasing heat. No sooner had he turned the hose on and started spraying the plants in their garden with a light mists then Sunshine was up and racing towards him. He snapped and bit at the stream of water, darting in and out. Bob quickly got distracted from his watering and began to chase Sunshine around with the hose. Eventually he was exhausted and Sunshine collapsed onto the ground, dripping wet but looking incredibly happy. Bob looked at the dog, saw how he was just lying there, no longer panting as he had been earlier, and then looked at Charlie, a smile spreading across his face.

"Oh no!" Charlie said quickly, "No way!"

"Come on," Bob said, turning the hose pipe off, "You've always wanted one,"

"But we just got the garden how we like it," Charlie whined, "Where would we put it?"

"Over there," Bob said, pointing towards a patch of land at the end of the garden.

It was bare, no grass or plants growing. No matter what the couple put down, how much fertilizer they used or how much water they put into the ground nothing would grow there. They'd begun to consider getting some expert to come and check it out. At the moment it was just a big patch of dusty brown earth that turned to mud whenever it rained.

"It's perfect," Bob said and he grinned.

***

It didn't take the two men long to finally get a small pond built on the barren patch of earth. They called in a few builders from nearby and within two days the hole was dug out, the lining placed in and the filter working. It was filled in a matter of hours. By the time that Sunshine returned, after a weekend that was spent with Ben and Mark and a brief visit to Ma and Pop, there was a sparkling pond at the end of the garden that he loved to run around in. He barely greeted Bob and Charlie before he raced off and plunged into the water.

Lulu however wouldn't go near it. All weekend they were trying to tempt the little gray dog into the pond, particularly at midday when all she seemed able to do was lie on the deck and pant from the heat. Bob went so far as to carry her to the very edge and set her down, nudging her to leap in. She wouldn't and when Bob picked her up and tried to place her in the water she yelped and writhed violently, trying to escape his clutches. The two men gave up and began to think that it was a wasted effort.

They were so happy when Sunshine raced into the pond without hesitation and began to swim around in the cool water. Lulu trotted over to the edge but still wouldn't go in. They laughed when Sunshine clambered out and shook himself dry, covering Lulu with water to her intense displeasure. She raced away, yelping and whining. She hid in the house and wouldn't come out again. Sunshine sat by the door, watching his friend but she seemed to be snubbing him so he eventually left, heading to Old Man Joe's although the two men didn't know it. Bear would probably play with him if Lulu wouldn't, was the thought going through Bailey's mind.

It took another day before Lulu would come out of the house and when Sunshine visited them he walked up to her hesitantly, as he did the first time that they met. She eventually barked and the two dogs began to race around as they usually did. Things seemed back to normal. When it got hot Sunshine leapt into the pond and splashed around in it before lying down in the shallow area, head resting clear of the water on the bank. Lulu sat nearby but would come no closer. Sunshine lay there, happily dozing, cool in the water despite the blistering sun. Lulu however was panting and the way that she kept glancing at Sunshine, cool and happy, seemed to be a lot like jealousy to the two men who watched the dogs from inside the coolness of their house.

Sunshine didn't give up trying to get Lulu to play in the pond with him. Day after day he returned and after the two dogs played together he would race into the pond and lay in the water for a while, cooling off until he could play again. He was never able to, Lulu was always too hot to race around, chasing him as they did earlier in the day. He was unhappy with this fact and he knew that Lulu was too. But he continued to try, lying in the shallows with her nearby.

Each day Lulu laid a little closer to him. Sometimes she would go to the very edge and the two men would watch with bated breath to see if she would jump in. She never did but she started to drink the cool water of the pool and that seemed to cool her enough to play with Sunshine some more but just for a little while.

Time passed and the pattern repeated itself, day after day. The spring turned into summer and the days grew hotter and longer. Then one day Charlie grabbed Bob's arm and pointed at the pond.

"Look!" he gasped sharply.

Lulu stood in the shallows, the water covering her feet. Sunshine lay nearby, watching her closely. She went no further in but she seemed much cooler and for the first time since the heat started she was able to play with Sunshine after his swim. It didn't last long and within an hour or so she was once more laying in the shade of the deck, lapping up water and panting hard to try and stay cool. The two men slumped in disappointment but realized that their dog made a major advancement and was possibly beginning to conquer her fear of water.

***

It was the barking that scared the two men and made them race to the deck. It sounded different, far away from the house, and there was a lot of splashing coming from the pond. They thought that another dog appeared, one that was less friendly than Sunshine. What they saw though made them stare in amazement.

Lulu was actually swimming in the pond, racing in and out of the water and chasing Sunshine in circles within the pond itself. Her coat was soaking and every time she left the water she would shake herself dry before moments later she leapt in again, determined to catch her quarry.

"Oh my gosh," Charlie said slowly, "She's actually doing it!"

"She's swimming," Bob said in amazement, "She's really swimming in the water."

The two men hugged each other tightly as they watched the two dogs playing in the water.

Sunshine was patient with Lulu spending day after day laying in the shallows while she paddled. He was determined to show her that the water wasn't dangerous in the slightest. Each day Lulu went a little deeper into the pond but never any higher than the bottom of her belly. Now she was swimming, her little legs working hard as she paddled through the water. Bob and Charlie were filled with joy and slowly and quietly made their way outside to sit on the deck, watching their favorite animals.

After that day Sunshine and Lulu would spend hours racing in and out of the pond. They would plunge in, chasing each other through the water before dashing out again, shaking themselves dry and chasing each other on dry land. They spent more and more time in the pond as the year passed into high summer and the days were the hottest in recent memory. Bob admitted one day to Charlie that he was a little jealous that the dogs could just go for a swim and cool off. Charlie pointed out that Bob could always join them in the pond and they laughed together.

The couple happily spent many hours together as they watched Lulu and Sunshine racing in and out of the water, splashing and barking and having fun. Their little family may not have been accepted or well-liked by the residents of The Hill but they were happy and shared love among themselves and that was what was important. They were used to Sunshine's ways, how he would come and go when it pleased him but whenever he did come he would stay for hours, playing with Lulu and letting the two men smother him with kisses and cuddles when it wasn't too hot for him.

Still Sunshine wanted more adventures and to make more friends. So he started spending a little less time at his favorite places and started to explore through the woods of The Hill more. If he wanted to make friends with everyone on The Hill it was what he needed to do. And any day he didn't want to explore he could go and spend time with the people and dogs that he loved, enjoying playing with them and basking in the love that they gave him.

Chapter 6

The Dog Catcher

One day as Bailey walked back from Charlie and Bob's house, following the road, he heard the sound of a car engine. It was a big sound, loud and rumbling. Bailey heard it a few times before but he always ran and hid from it. Mark and Ben warned him to stay away from the road, whenever they took him for a walk on his lead they kept themselves between him and the dirt track. Bailey saw the way the big metal creatures swept past, the cloud of dust they kicked up behind them and how fast they travelled. The wind they created ruffled his fur and at one point the wind threatened to knock Bailey off his feet.

Today, as Bailey's ears perked up and he heard the sound of the engine he was too tired to move into the undergrowth. He was swimming in the pond and racing around the garden with Lulu all day. The car came closer and Bailey saw that it was a van type vehicle. He had seen it several times before, moving around The Hill and stopping from time to time. The man in it seemed to hate dogs, he would stop and collect any that were wandering around without their owners. Bailey saw it for himself, the way that the man in the big van would slowly get the loose dogs to come closer before suddenly grabbing them and dragging them to the back of his van. Bailey's sharp ears picked up on the sound of whining, the whimpering of other dogs inside the van. The man collected dogs and took them away.

Bailey saw the van getting closer and wondered why the man collected the dogs and where he took them after he caught them. He knew it couldn't be anywhere too bad, he often saw the other dogs wandering around again with their owners. But as the van got closer Bailey could smell sadness, misery and a deep scent of suffering. Wherever the man took the other dogs may not have been horrible but it was not a good place, it didn't smell like a good place.

Bailey stopped and sniffed the air as the van started to slow. It didn't smell as sad today but the scent lingered. He waggled his tail as the van finally stopped and the man climbed out. He looked like a nice man but there was something strange about him, something that wasn't good. Bailey's tail stopped wagging and slowly dropped down. The man reached into the van and pulled out a stick with a loop hanging from the end. The man clutched it with both hands and slowly stepped towards Bailey. The yellow dog saw that stick before, he saw the way that the loop went around the necks of other dogs and then let the man drag them towards the van. Bailey barked and turned around before he raced into the forest behind him.

The man cursed and raced after him. Bailey kept barking, deciding that he did have enough energy to play this fun new game with a new person who could become his friend. He spun and ran through the undergrowth, barking as he went. He could hear the man behind him, shouting and cursing as his stick with the loop got caught on the bushes that littered the ground. Suddenly there was a great crash from behind Bailey and he heard the man who followed him fall to the ground. Bailey twisted and ran quickly back. He burst out through some bushes to find the man knee deep in thick mud. He barked and sat at the very edge of the hole that the man fell into. The man waved his stick at Bailey but he couldn't reach the yellow dog. Bailey barked, amused by the funny expression on the man's face before he stood, turned and disappeared back into the forest. He would have to play with his new friend another day.

The man stood there, watching as the dog disappeared into the bushes. He could hear the rustling of leaves slowly fading away until he was completely alone with only the sounds of the birds singing and the leaves blowing.

"Hey!" the man shouted, "Hey you! Get back here! Stupid dog, come back!"

The man just stood there, realizing that the dog had no intention of coming back. He sighed and began trying to pull himself free of the thick mud at the bottom of the hole.

***

A few days later Bailey had found a new house. He'd traveled further than ever before and finally found a new house that looked promising for finding a new friend. It was a small house, much smaller than Ben and Mark's house. But it was clearly loved and it smelled like a home, fresh baking and meat. Bailey slowly made his way down the drive, inching closer to the house. He could hear sounds coming from inside the house, from around the back and he edged his way around the side of the house, keeping close to the building. Then he smelled a scent he recognized. It was the same smell of sadness and suffering that hung around the van he found those days before. This was the home of the man in the van.

For a moment Bailey considered turning around and running. The run in with the man in the van was fun but there was still something about the scent of that van and the way that the man looked at him that made the fur on his back stand on end. But then he heard the sound of a woman laughing and Bailey wanted to know who it was. Her laughter sounded real, loving and warm. It reminded him of the way that Ma laughed whenever he did something she thought was silly. Bailey realized that he really wanted to see who this person was. So he kept walking along the edge of the house and around to the back.

The back door was open and he could see a woman moving around inside the kitchen. She was talking to someone, a bar of black plastic tucked between her shoulder and her head.

"Honey, please can we have a dog?" she said quietly, "There's so many dogs out there that need a home, and we can give them one."

Bailey could make out the sounds of a voice from the end but he couldn't hear the words. The woman didn't seem to look too happy with what she could hear.

"But I get so lonely here on my own," she said quietly. "I just want something to keep me company while you're out all day finding dogs to take to the pound,"

The woman frowned as whoever was on the end of the black bar carried on speaking. She eventually sighed.

"Ok, ok," she said quietly. "I'll stop going on about it."

She took a flour covered hand and moved the black bar away from her face. The buttons beeped as she pressed something on it and then plonked the bar on the counter she stood beside. Bailey moved closer and sat at the doorway. He watched as she carried on moving her hands around inside a beige bowl. She seemed sad all of a sudden, her mouth was turned down and Bailey could practically smell it on her. He didn't like how upset she was, she seemed nice when she was smiling and happy. He inched closer to the door and lay at the threshold. The woman sighed again.

Bailey couldn't help himself. He sighed as well. The woman looked up quickly and gasped when she saw the yellow dog lying on her doorstep. The bowl fell from her hands where she was clutching it and rattled on the counter top. Bailey sat up and dropped his jaw open, hanging his tongue from his mouth. His tail wagged happily and he cocked his head to one side. The woman seemed to recompose herself and she wiped her hands clean on a towel that hung from her belt. She slowly made her way around the counter and moved closer to Bailey. She held out her hand and crouched down as she got nearer to him.

"Hey you," she said softly. "Where'd you come from?"

She finally knelt down beside Bailey and started to scratch behind his ears. He leaned into her hand and his tail wagged harder and harder. The woman smiled and tickled him harder.

"Aren't you a friendly fellow," she said softly, "What's your name hey? I'm Barbara."

She searched his neck for a collar but found nothing. Barbara bit her lip and looked over her shoulder towards the front door. Her husband wouldn't like this. It was his job to collect dogs just like this one and here one sat right on their very doorstep. Bailey yipped softly and butted his head against her hand. She turned back to him and smiled gently. Bailey's head relaxed against her hand completely and he started to expose his neck while his eyes slid shut. He was clearly enjoying the attention that she was giving him and she couldn't help but laugh.

Then suddenly, without any warning the yellow dog sat up and looked towards the driveway. His ears perked up as he heard something and he gave a small yip before he quickly stood and ran away, back through the kitchen door. Barbara stood and watched him go. She followed the yellow dog around the edge of the house and saw her husband's van coming up their driveway.

***

Officer Henderson was tired and a little muddy. He spent most of the day tracking down sightings of the yellow dog that evaded capture a few days before. He found nothing and only scratched legs and a sore back to show for his troubles. There were leaves in his hair and his trousers were covered in mud after he fell into the hole that he discovered last time. The sightings of the yellow dog led him all over The Hill but after a few of them turned out to be pranks he began to wonder whether the residents even wanted him to find the loose dog that was clearly terrorizing the neighborhood. He supposed it was understandable given that he took so many dogs to the pound in his career as a dog catcher, many of them simply lost by careless owners. But he was doing his job and following orders. If owners couldn't be bothered to keep their animals within their own land then it was his duty to collect them and take them away somewhere where they couldn't cause trouble.

As he pulled up to the house he saw Barbara appearing around the side of the house and a splash of yellow fur just in front of her. He slammed on his brakes, pulling the van to a screeching halt, and climbed out, quickly grabbing his stick as he did so.

"Hey you!" he shouted as soon as he was clear of the van, "Get back here you!"

The yellow dog, the very same one he was chasing all day was here on his property and he'd be darned if he let the creature escape him again. He raced after the dog that barked, wiggled and ran away, lolloping through the grass of his front garden. The dog ran circles around him and he could hear Barbara cheering and laughing from the side of the house. He glanced over and she was holding herself up against the wall, clutching her stomach with her free hand as she laughed so hard that tears ran down her face.

"Stop laughing and help me!" he shouted. The dog darted towards him and jolted away again at the last moment, "Hey you, get back here!"

The dog barked and took off down the driveway. Officer Henderson tried to catch him but he twisted too quickly and toppled to the ground, the loop of his stick twisted around his feet. Barbara laughed even harder at that, practically cackling with glee. Officer Henderson tried to climb to his feet but they were tangled and he simply fell over once more. That sent Barbara into further wails of laughter. By the time that Henderson got himself free of his stick the yellow dog vanished again and there were no signs he was there.

"What were you thinking?" he snapped, turning towards his wife who was still laughing, "That dog could have been dangerous and there you go following it around,"

"He's about as dangerous as a lamb," Barbara said between laughs, "He came right up to the door and let me cuddle him,"

"He's a loose dog Barb," Henderson said firmly, "Who knows what kind of diseases he's carrying around,"

"He's harmless," Barbara said firmly, "And clearly he's well looked after. There wasn't a bit of old dirt in his fur,"

"You don't know that!" Henderson said, "You don't know where he's come from or who he belongs to. What if he just snapped and tore your throat out? Then what would you do?"

"Well I'd probably be dead," Barbara said snidely. "Now go shower George, you're covered in mud again,"

"Because I've been chasing that darn dog all around the countryside," Henderson muttered as he took off his boots at the front door, "And then it turns out he's been here the entire time,"

"Oh go shower!" Barbara said, snapping her tea towel at him, "You smell worse than some of those dogs you find."

George smiled softly at his wife and made his way up the stairs. He didn't mean to be short with her but he was all too aware of the dangers that loose dogs posed to people who didn't know them. He'd seen it too many times when he lived in the city, the results of dog attacks were there to see everywhere he looked. It was why he'd dragged Barbara out to The Hill in the first place, to get away from it. Now there they were with a loose dog wandering into his very home. George shook his head and sighed, reaching the bathroom and shoving his muddy clothes into the laundry basket.

***

Bailey liked the house he'd found, even if the dog catcher lived there. He decided that he really enjoyed playing the game with the man where he tried to catch Bailey but Bailey just ran away. He liked the way that Barbara would always laugh whenever the dog catcher fell over. He liked the way she would cheer and whoop as Bailey always escaped and disappeared into the forests again. He began to realize that his name at this house wasn't Bailey, it was 'Hey You'. That was all he was ever called around there. The dog catcher shouted it and he could hear anger in the man's voice. But Barbara said it softly and kindly, with a smile on her face. She would always cuddle him and sneak him scraps of bacon but he could never stay for long.

The dog catcher, Officer Henderson, would always reappear just as Hey You started to get comfortable in the house and Hey You would have to race away before Officer Henderson could catch him. Those chases were fun, even if the dog catcher didn't seem to see it that way.

One evening, just as the sun came out from behind some clouds Hey You was lounging on the porch by Barbara's feet. She was tickling his stomach and he was so wrapped up in the pleasure he was feeling that he didn't even hear Officer Henderson driving towards the house. The only warning he got was when the van door slammed shut.

"Hey You!" Officer Henderson shouted, "Stay where you are, it's time to come with me."

George didn't stop, he didn't even pause. Instead he raced towards the house, arms and legs working madly. His stick with the loop was in his hand, the loop bobbed up and down as the stick waved with every step. Hey You scrambled to stand on his paws and barked. He waited until George was at the very top of the porch steps and making his way towards where Hey You and Barbara sat before he ran, dodged around the man and jumped down the steps. George cursed and spun on his heels. He almost lost his balance but he flung out his arm and caught himself just in time. He cursed again when he tried to move forwards and realized that his looped stick was caught between the railings of the porch.

Hey You barked from where he was stood on the front garden, his tail wagging madly. He wanted to wait for George to get free so that he could continue their game. Eventually George managed to pull his stick free, almost falling to the floor at the sudden freedom, before he started to run down the stairs towards Hey You. Hey You didn't wait, as soon as George's foot hit the ground he raced off again, around the side of the house and towards the outbuildings. He could hear George running after him, the man's boots pounding heavily on the hard earth. Hey You barked and leapt into the air as he ran. He darted suddenly, away from the path that he was following and ducked into the cool dimness of the Henderson's barn.

George followed after the yellow dog and smiled. The animal was cornered now. He reached the doorway and looked into the barn, peering through the darkness within. He could hear the yellow dog panting, could see its bright fur shifting among the shadows. He reached out for the doors and slide them shut, turning his back for just a moment. When he turned back Hey You stood in the very center of the barn, tail wagging madly. George slammed the bar in place, holding the doors shut, and advanced towards the dog, pole held out in front of him. Hey You barked and scrambled to his feet. Then without warning the yellow dog, now brown in the darkness of the barn, turned and raced off further into the shadows.

George peered through the shadows, trying to see anything that might give him a clue as to where the dog went. He could hear it shuffling somewhere within the barn. Then everything went quiet as he stepped on a creaking floorboard. The dog started scrambling, its claws dragging against something. Then, everything fell silent once more. Light seemed to stream into the barn, suddenly brighter for some reason. Then George heard a scraping and scratching sound from the door outside and the doors shook as something heavy crashed against them.

George cursed and raced towards them. He shook the doors, pushing and pulling but they would not budge. The dog locked him in!

***

About a week later George Henderson returned home from work and found the yellow dog was there again. He was still furious about the fact that Hey You managed to escape through a hole in the barn wall and then proceeded to knock the wooden bar across the front of the doors. It took Barbara over half an hour to get him out, she was so shaken up with laughter and the rest of the week she would burst into giggles every time she remembered the incident.

This time George was silent as he climbed out of his van and quietly shut the door behind him. The yellow dog was lying by the side of the drive around to the back of the house. Hey You was enjoying the sunshine and from the stillness of his tail he was clearly asleep. As carefully as he could George crept towards Hey You, holding the pole out, ready to slip the loop around the dog's neck. He was only a few feet away, moments from catching the dog at last. Then suddenly the dog looked up, leapt to its feet and took off.

George cursed and raced after Hey You, no longer making any effort to keep quiet. The dog knew he was there so there was no point. Barbara came around the side of the house just as Hey You raced past, closely followed by her husband. She watched them go, her mouth hanging open in surprise. Then she slowly jogged after the pair as they continued to race around the small holding that the Henderson's lived on. She started laughing as Hey You ran back and forth across the paddock, twisting this way and that. George tried his best to chase after the fast, agile creature but Hey You was just quicker and better at escaping.

Barbara's jaw dropped open as George almost got the loop around Hey You's neck but suddenly the dog put on a burst of speed and tore ahead of the dog catcher. She smiled and clapped, unable to help herself. She really wanted the dog to escape. When George almost caught Hey You again before Hey You raced off and then the pattern repeated itself she realized that Hey You was playing with George, deliberately leading him on a merry chase while never actually allowing himself to be caught. She leaned against the fence and watched the two running around.

George was panting for breath even as he continued to run after the yellow dog. His heart leapt each time he almost got that loop around Hey You's neck but the dog would always speed ahead just before he managed it. He was growing impatient. He'd almost managed to catch the dog three times already but it kept speeding off every time he almost caught it. The grass was getting torn up the more that he ran around, the dirt turning to mud as his feet pounded the damp grass. His feet were starting to slip and once or twice he almost went over, only catching himself at the last moment with a hand in the mud. He was determined. As long as Hey You remained in his sight he would catch the dog. But first he needed to catch his breath.

He stopped running and leaned his elbows on his knees. He breathed hard and deep, his lungs filling over and over. Sweat poured down his face and settled into the cloth under his arms. He heard a bark and looked up, still panting. Hey You sat near him, just out of reach of his pole. The dog was looking at him, head tilted to one side, tongue hanging out and tail wagging. George glared at the dog but it just looked at him. His heart slowed to a steady rhythm but still he leaned on his elbows. Hey You barked again and then George leapt forwards with the pole outstretched.

Hey You yelped in surprise and darted away but its tail was wagging madly. He began to race away and George ran after him. The dog leapt and bounded through the long grass, covering wide sections of earth with a single bound. George simply ran after him, one foot in front of the other. Suddenly there was no ground beneath his feet and he was stumbling down a small ditch. He landed in a small pond of water with a loud splash.

"Jeeze!" he shouted when his head broke the water at last. "You little…. Ahh!"

George cried out and threw the stick at the dog which sat on the edge of the hole, looking down at him. The stick missed by a mile and George was just left staring at the dog. The water came up to his waist and it was chilly. Water dripped down his face and into his eyes. He shivered slightly as the breeze pressed the wet clothes against him. He could hear Barbara laughing her head off in the distance.

"I found the pond!" George shouted, "That one that was on the plans but we could never find."

George glared at Hey You one last time before turning and climbing out of the pond on the opposite bank. He clambered to his feet and slowly walked away, his shoes squelching as he walked. He wouldn't be chasing Hey You until he dried out a little and changed his shoes. The yellow dog barked and disappeared off into the woods. George found himself waving a hand towards the dog.

***

George no longer hated Hey You as much as he did in the beginning. If anything he found that he enjoyed the chases that Hey You put him through, they were fun and challenging, the yellow dog showed more skill and intelligence than any other dog Henderson tried to catch. In fact Hey You was the only dog he had not captured and taken to the pound. He also enjoyed how happy and amused Barbara seemed to be whenever Hey You came to visit or whenever George was forced to chase him around their property.

George made it a point to only chase the dog when he saw him, no longer did the dog catcher set out to track down the dog and take him to the pound. If Hey You was there on his property and allowed himself to get caught then George would catch him but otherwise that was as far as their conflict went. As time passed and as their chases continued George began to no longer think of the dog as Hey You, instead he started to call the dog Spirit because there was such spirit in him.

***

Bailey knew he could never actually stay at the house where the dog catcher lived. He wasn't welcome there when the dog catcher was around although his wife seemed to like him. Bailey enjoyed the games they would play though, as he ran from the dog catcher and let himself almost be caught several times. He knew that no matter how bored he may have been there was still a chance of excitement at the Henderson's.

Bailey still wanted to make new friends that gave him the chance to have exciting adventures. So he continued to explore The Hill, seeing the neighbors nearby and hoping to find someone new to play with each and every day. He continued to visit old friends and the new friends that he hoped he would one day be making.

Chapter 7

Marianne

For a while Bailey decided to stay close to his homes with Ben and Mark and Bob and Charlie and Ma and Pop. He shared his time between the homes, staying with Ben and Mark most of the time and now and then staying with Ma and Pop out in their garden when it grew too hot. He played with Bob and Charlie and Lulu in the pond. From time to time he would pay a visit to Officer Henderson's home and play with Barbara. He would run away from George and lead him to all sorts of trouble. He enjoyed his life and he enjoyed his freedom. Sometimes, when the days were long and too hot to think about even leaving the coolness of Mark's house he wondered whether or not he should find a new friend or two to play with.

Eventually Bailey decided to go and explore. Ma and Pop went back to Rochester to visit Amanda, Bob and Charlie took Lulu to a place called Virginia for a holiday and Ben and Mark were still working in the city for much of the week. So Bailey found himself alone and bored. Even

Old Man Joe was busy with Bear, traveling around the state selling his honey at farmer's markets. So Bailey was bored, no one to play with and no one to visit. He decided, as he woke up when Ben and Mark left, that he would spend the day trying to find a new friend. It was better than just lying around and doing nothing.

So Bailey set off into the woods, following the scent of a new house that came from further down The Hill. It was a nice scent and it reminded him of Mark. He remembered the parties that Mark would throw from time to time, when Ben was off somewhere else. People would come and lots of them would give him cuddles and play with him. They would, by the end, smell strongly of grains and grapes and the scent would linger around the house for many days afterwards. That was similar to what he could smell now although it was only light and there wasn't quite the depth of muskiness to the scent. But it was gently being blown towards Mark's house and Bailey wanted to know where it was coming from.

The people who smelled like that at Mark's house were always very friendly but they acted a little strangely from time to time. Bailey wondered whether this house would have nice friendly people in it. He made his way through the forest and as he got closer to the new house and the smell got stronger he started to remember things. He remembered Mark going around to the house, he followed him, and Mark started shouting at the woman who lived there. She was sad, Bailey remembered that, and she yelled back at Mark as strongly as he yelled at her. Then Bailey remembered the woman coming around to that house as there were lots of people around. They were shooting guns into the air and the noise hurt Bailey's ears a little. It turned out that the woman didn't like it either, she was really angry and started to shout and rage at Mark. The people left soon after, when men came in a big white car with flashing lights.

Bailey saw the house through the trees and stopped at the very edge of the forest. He wondered whether he should go there, Mark and the woman didn't seem to like each other and maybe Bailey making friends with the lady would make things even worse between the two than they were already. Then again it could make things better between them. Maybe if they found out that they shared a love of Bailey they might get along. Then again none of Bailey's families knew about each other and Bailey liked it that way. Bailey decided and stepped out from the trees. He started to head towards the little white house surrounded by flowers.

***

Marianne sighed and sipped at her coffee. She slowly flipped through the newspaper that was in front of her. She didn't know what to do with herself. It was one of her days off and she was trying to find a way of entertaining herself. Normally she would be helping her clients improve the homes that they rented from her but everything there was done. And her usual work at the vineyard was over for now, the off season having come and she was not needed until the next tourist season started in a few months. So, with little else to do Marianne was finding herself bored. Her husband passed away a few years before and until now she had not found anything to keep herself busy. Now she had nothing to entertain herself. She wondered if it was too early for a glass of wine or two and glanced at the clock. It was still too early.

She leaned her head on her hand and stared out through the window and into the garden. It was all green out there and the flowers were in full bloom. They swayed gently in the breeze. Briefly, as she watched the garden, she wondered why she never made any friends on The Hill. Even when her husband was alive they were mostly cut off from everyone. They just didn't really like to talk to people, they didn't know how to talk to people. Now, without her husband Marianne rarely went out. She had a few friends at the vineyard and spent time with them but for the most part but she tended to live a solitary life.

The arguments with the neighbors hadn't been fun either. She hoped, when she saw the building going on nearby that she would finally have some friends nearby. The older gentleman seemed nice enough but the younger man made her uncomfortable and despite the distance between their two houses the sound carried and the young man liked to throw loud and raucous parties. She couldn't help but feel jealous of the number of friends the younger man had. For the most part the noise just annoyed her and the loud shouting traveled well in the stillness of the night. Trying to sleep on those nights was near impossible and once or twice she was forced to go around and yell at them. It got even worse when they started firing off guns and she was forced to call the police.

Marianne admitted she felt a little guilty about that. It may have been overreacting and it definitely made things even worse between herself and the two men but she felt, at the time, that it was the right thing to do. People couldn't just go around firing guns off at all hours of the night. Still, it destroyed any chance of ever becoming friends with Ben, even if she wanted to. She sighed again, as there was another reminder of the fact that she was completely alone. The garden was completely empty, not even an animal ran through the flowers. She closed her eyes and yawned. She still needed to find something to keep herself amused and occupied.

When she opened her eyes she spotted something in the garden. It was a medium sized creature with yellow fur. Marianne squinted and leaned in closer to the window. It was a dog, a yellow Labrador. She smiled gently and waved at the dog. It walked towards the house, tail wagging madly. It barked at her. Her smile grew even wider. John always wanted a dog, a Labrador in particular. And now, just when she was thinking about him here was a yellow Labrador. Marianne felt it was a sign and she climbed to her feet.

The dog didn't move as she walked to the back door and opened it. When she stepped outside the dog came closer to her, his tail wagging high and fast. Then, just as her feet settled on the grass, Marianne's little dogs came tumbling out of the house. She cried out and tried to stop them, worried that they would end up hurt. But nothing happened. If anything the yellow dog seemed happy to see them. He began to race around happily with them, the group tumbling around his feet and all of them barking together. She laughed hard as they bounded around the garden, the yellow dog tripping over his own feet and the dogs that surrounded him. They rolled around together, the small dogs jumping up and down on top of the yellow dog whenever he fell to the ground. They wiggled around together in a pool of fur.

Marianne laughed and sat on the steps. She watched the dogs enjoying themselves and listened to the happy yaps of the little dogs and the new yellow dog. Eventually her dogs fell down to the ground and lay there panting for breath. The yellow dog wasn't as out of breath as they were and instead came over to Marianne. He approached her slowly, waiting until she placed her hand on his head. Then he scrambled a little closer and rested his head on her knee. She laughed and scratched her fingers through the soft fur.

"Hello Love," she said quietly, "You're a friendly fellow aren't you?"

The yellow dog made no response. Instead he rested his head on her knee more firmly, leaning more of his weight against her and his eyes slid shut as she scratched behind his ears. His tail wagged even harder.

"You came at just the right time," she said to him softly, "I was starting to get lonely,"

The yellow dog said nothing, his tail continued to wag and Marianne continued to tickle him around the ears and neck.

***

Marianne adored it when the yellow dog came around. She took to calling him Love whenever she saw him. It was another sunny morning when Love came around. As soon as Love stepped out from between the trees her dogs tumbled out from the house and raced across the lawn. They barked madly as they scrambled all around Love. Marianne walked out of the house, leaving behind the bottle of wine that she was about to pour. She settled herself on the porch and watched the dogs playing together. For the first time in a long time she felt something close to happiness filling her heart. It left her warm inside and almost made her want to cry.

Love kept coming around for a few weeks, almost like clockwork. He would come out of the trees, every time and the dogs would all go running out to greet him. Marianne would watch them all playing in the garden as she went about her business in the house. There wasn't much to do so she spent most of the time that Love was around just sitting at the garden table and watching the dogs play together. Once or twice, whenever Love didn't come round as he usually did, Marianne found herself reaching for the wine a little earlier than usually.

He would always end up staying the night when he came to visit. She never planned it that way but Love stayed for the entire day, playing with her dogs, joining them all on a walk through the back roads. As the night drew in and everyone went inside Love followed them in. The dogs all settled in their beds, the little rounded pillowed things that were scattered around the house. Marianne expected Love to head home once his little dog friends began to snore but instead he settled by her feet and begged to be petted. She obliged him and read her book quietly. Once or twice she almost got up to get some wine but whenever she would move away or stop stroking Love he would turn his head and look at her with disapproving brown eyes. She couldn't help but smile and settle herself down on the sofa again.

Today was just the same as it always was. The dogs were tumbling around the garden and Marianne settled into a comfortable chair on the porch to read her book and watch the dogs play. She found herself lost in the words and was surprised when she felt a cold wet nose pressed against her bare leg. She squealed in shock and looked down. It was Love with a random red ball in his mouth. She leaned forward and Love dropped the ball in her hand.

"Where did you find this Love?" she asked quietly.

There was no response from Love but to stare at Marianne. She waved the ball at him and he stood up. His mouth dropped open and his tongue rolled out as he smiled.

"Oh you want to play do you?" she asked quietly. She waved it around and Love watched the ball move. "Oh you do don't you! Ok, here you go Love!"

She tossed the ball across the garden and Love took off after it, tearing across the lawn. She laughed as he went and tumbled across the grass, he was so excited about the ball that he was tripping over his own feet. Her dogs just stayed where they were, watching in confusion as their friend ran after a round red thing. She wasn't surprised in their disinterest. She'd tried to get them to play fetch with the ball several times in the past, it was why she had the ball in the first place. But they didn't want to fetch the ball had lay in the garden, undisturbed since then. Now Love found it and was determined to play, at least judging by the way he returned and shoved the slobbery ball into her hands.

Marianne grimaced at the sensation but drew her arm back and tossed the ball again. Love took off after it but this time some of Marianne's dogs followed him. They didn't seem interested in the ball but they seemed to be curious about what Love was doing. Love snuffled through the flower bed and eventually his head popped up from among the flowers, ball in mouth. The other dogs came around him and sniffed at the ball. He eventually lifted his head above the dogs around him and trotted towards Marianne. She smiled and reached out for the ball. When she took it from Love's mouth the other dogs leapt around her, jumping for the ball themselves.

Marianne tossed the ball and this time all of the dogs raced after it, Love included. They scrambled around each other trying to get the ball. Marianne laughed and laughed as they all tried to reach the ball first and tumbled around each other to get it before the others. At last they were playing fetch, Love actually taught them to play fetch! She wondered what other tricks they could learn from this clearly intelligent dog.

***

Over time Love became another part of the family, just another dog in Marianne's pack. He taught her dogs tricks, just as she wondered whether he would. By watching Love Marianne's dogs learned how to roll over, sit, and lie down. Some were slower than others, granted, but they all learned those tricks eventually and Marianne loved watching them get smarter and cleverer. And she just loved having Love around. She always had a cookie waiting for him, every time that he turned up. Her husband always loved peanut butter cookies. Now she found herself buying them again.

She couldn't figure out why she felt that she should get them for Love. She'd just been shopping one morning, picking up a few things for her meals and she'd spotted Ben and Mark down another aisle. She'd dipped away into an aisle, one she tended to avoid. As she watched the two men wandering around, waiting for them to pass her by, her eyes landed on the cookies that lined the shelves. Before she could even think about it she'd picked up a pack and put them in her basket. It wasn't until she got home that she realized she'd actually gone ahead and bought them. She thought she put them back on the shelf.

Marianne was confused and worried about what to do with them. She didn't want to throw them away that would be a huge waste. She never liked to waste food or money and throwing away cookies would be a really big waste. She stood at the counter, holding the cookies in one hand that hung by her hand. Then she felt a wet nose pressed against the hand holding the cookies and she jumped in shock. When she looked down she saw Love looking at her, tongue hanging from his mouth as usual. She smiled at him.

"Do you want a cookie?" she asked him kindly, "John always loved them,"

Love stared up at her, eyes locked on the cookies. She smiled and opened the cookies. She held it out to Love and he gently took it from her. He crunched it down and swallowed before he looked up at her again.

"Ah ah ah," she said firmly, wagging a finger at her, "Only the one for you, can't have you getting all fat and overweight can we."

Love whined gently as she put the cookies up into one of the cupboards. She smiled and rubbed his head gently. He licked her hand, trying to get all of the crumbs from her skin. She laughed and crouched down in front of him. She rubbed hard at his fur, making him wiggle from side to side and he wagged his tail hard. He closed his eyes and leaned into the rubs.

***

Marianne tossed and turned in her bed. She was trying to sleep but realized Mark was throwing another party, which was what they were at the supermarket earlier. Now it was late in the evening, she was trying to sleep but all she could hear was the pounding of music and the occasional shot gun sound. She groaned and sat up. She brought her knees up and leaned her elbows on them, putting her head in her hands. The music seemed to get a little louder every minute that passed.

"Why is it every time I have work in the morning he throws a party?" she muttered to herself. "I ought to give him a piece of my mind."

She climbed from the bed and shivered as her bare feet hit the coldness of the wooden floor. Love looked up from his spot at the end of the bed and whined gently. Marianne looked over from where she was pulling her robe on and walked over to the bed. She put her hand on Love's head and rubbed gently.

"It's ok Love," she murmured quietly, "I'm not going to go and do anything, don't you worry."

Instead of getting dressed as she initially intended she kept her robe wrapped tightly around herself and slipped on a pair of warm socks. She padded through the house in near silence. It seemed quieter downstairs. The lower floor was below the level of the trees which meant that most of the sound by the nearby house was being blocked off by the massive tree trunks. Her dogs didn't seem to be bothered by the noise, even with their sensitive hearing. Instead they were just lying there in strange positions, snoring away. Then she heard the ticking of toenails on the wooden floors. She looked down and realized that Love followed her down.

In the kitchen she turned on the light and headed over to the fridge. She initially reached for a bottle of wine but Love's tail bumped against her leg. She smiled down at the dog and absently put the wine back, instead picking up the jug of milk. After heating it in a cup and taking it into the living room with her she settled on the sofa and returned to reading the book she started earlier that evening. Love hopped up onto the seat beside her, turned around a few times before settling down. His head rested on her knees so she could pet his fur and play with his ears. He groaned in contentment and she smiled even as her eyes raced over the words.

The music was still pounding slightly in the background but Marianne realized that it was no longer bothering her as much. It was just background noise, something that she was able to block out as she read. If anything it seemed to be helping her concentrate on the words on the page. She smiled and put her book down. She remembered how these evening used to go, when she was woken up or kept awake by the thumping of music and the loud shouts. She would often spend hour after hour, steadily drinking down wine. That was usually why she went over to the other house and gave the young man who lived there a piece of her mind. She certainly wasn't sober when she called the police and she realized it the next morning with a predictable hangover.

Now the parties were less often and Marianne found that they didn't bother her as much as they once did. She no longer spent the evening drinking to get to sleep. Of course she drank entire bottles of wine on days when there weren't parties but even those stopped happening as often as they did before. She didn't feel like she needed them anymore. The noises of the parties would annoy her, as they would anyone, and she found herself getting irritated whenever she was woken up but she no longer went straight to the wine. Just like tonight she would find something else to drink, something warm and soothing, and then she would settle down and read until she was too tired to keep her eyes open. Usually there would be no chance of even the party noises keeping her awake and she'd fall asleep within moments of her head hitting the pillow.

The contented groan at her knee made her realize why she had such a massive change in attitude. It was all thanks to Love. She no longer felt so alone, she was reminded that just because she had no friends she wasn't alone and she could have a happy and fulfilling life without having to be surrounded by people. Sitting down with a book and Love's head on her knee left her much happy and healthier than sitting down with a bottle of wine, if not two. Not to mention her head felt better the next day too. If she wasn't hung-over she could play with her dogs and Love instead of hiding in the shadowed rooms of the house. She could take them for long walks and spend time enjoying their company. She could do things that she wanted to do, explore new hobbies that she never had the energy to do.

Her change in attitude towards her wine evenings led to a change in her health and her attitude. She was full of energy again, she felt about ten years younger. She could stay awake longer and she no longer found the excited yapping of her little dogs as annoying as they once did. The slightest things no longer bothered her, she didn't find herself flying into a rage at the drop of a hat. Gone were the headaches, the nausea, and the irritability. Things still confused her and scared her of course but now she was able to take them in her stride and after a few moments of calming deep breaths she continued on with what she was doing and it was all thanks to Love.

She leaned forward and placed a big kiss on his yellow head. His tongue wagged from his mouth and he leaned into the kiss, eyes pressed closed.

"Thank you Love." She murmured quietly.

The sound from the party died out and Marianne realized that her tiredness returned. She went to her room and left the downstairs in silence. Outside there was only the screeching of owls and the wind in the trees.

***

Mark looked up from his newspaper as Bailey trotted up the drive. It was early morning and despite the fact that it was the weekend he found himself awake fairly early. He'd tried to put off getting out of bed for as long as possible but he'd eventually forced himself to get up. Now he was downstairs in the kitchen, reading a paper. He happened to glance out of the window just as Bailey rounded the corner of the drive and started to head towards the house.

"Where have you been all night?" he muttered to himself.

He continued to get up and went to open the door. As soon as Bailey stepped into the house he shoved his nose into Mark's hand and wagged his tail. Mark ruffled Bailey's fur on his head and smiled at the yellow dog.

"So you've been at Ma and Pop's again?" Mark asked him. "You're going to forget where you really live one of these days."

Bailey wagged his tail hard before heading into the house further and settling down on the bed that Ben and Mark put down for him. He lay in the bed, licking his mouth and settled down to sleep. He hadn't been at Ma and Pop's like Mark thought. In fact he actually was at Marianne's house. He stayed over once or twice a month there and let Ben and Mark believe what they wanted. He had more friends than he ever expected and he loved them all dearly. And soon he would find even more, he hoped. Then would come new friends, just as he liked it.

Chapter 8

The Truck Driver

Bailey didn't like the big heavy truck that would come roaring along the road from time to time. It was loud and made the ground rumble. The smell from it was horrible and always made him want to sneeze. And the man who came out of it smelled just as bad. He was louder than the truck, Bailey never thought that was possible, and there was a strong smell of alcohol that lingered around him. It was always a stale smell of alcohol though, never as fresh as it smelled on Mark when he was having a party. It smelled more like Mark did a few days later but the man didn't moan and groan like Mark did. It just seemed to make him grumpier than normal.

Bailey always knew when the man and his truck were around The Hill. He could smell the scent in the wind. One time when he was on an adventure he saw the truck pull to a stop near Charlie and Bob's house. Lulu ran out on to the road, escaping from Charlie's grasp. For a moment Bailey almost came running out of the bushes to save his friend from the angry man that was climbing out of the truck but Charlie appeared and scooped the little dog up. But the man in the truck was still angry. A cigarette dangling from his mouth and started coming towards Charlie who was clutching Lulu's shaking body tightly. The man made himself seem big, Bailey recognized the move from when Shadow did it to him. But Bailey was just a puppy then and now he was full grown Shadow didn't do it anymore. This man didn't seem to care that Charlie was a grown man, he just started shouting and raving at the man and his dog.

Even when Bob came running down the drive it didn't help. If anything that man in the truck seemed to make himself even bigger and started shouting even more. He took the cigarette from his mouth and spat on the ground. Bailey sneezed in the bushes, the smell from the spit really was horrible and the wind was blowing it right towards where the yellow dog was hiding. The man kept shouting and Lulu started shaking and whimpering even more. Bailey wanted to rush out and help his friends, he really loved Lulu and Charlie and Bob.

"Get the heck out of here or I'm calling the police!" Bob eventually shouted.

He was waving a slim black box around and Bailey knew that was the special box that let people talk to each other and would bring the big men in the cars with flashing lights. He liked that box, the voices that came out of it always sounded like people he knew whenever Ben or Mark or Ma or Pop held it to one of his floppy ears.

The truck driver didn't seem to like it. He grumbled and snarled, almost as bad as the bear that Bailey chased away for Old Man Joe, but eventually turned around and climbed back into his truck. It pulled away from Charlie and Bob's driveway with a squeal of the tires and a cloud of sandy dust. It disappeared down the road and around the corner quickly. Bailey waited until the sound faded away before he leapt out of the bushes and raced across the road to his friends.

"Hello Sunshine," Charlie said softly.

He knelt down in front of Bailey and placed Lulu on the ground. She was still shaking, terrified and Bailey sniffed at her and licked her nose. She crept close to him, pressing herself against his side and whimpering. Bailey whimpered softly back and led her back towards Bob and Charlie's house. The two men followed behind them.

"It looks like you turned up just in time Sunshine," Bob said. "Lulu's probably really glad to see her friend."

There was no playing in the pond that day, nor was there any racing around the garden. The incident with the truck driver seemed to have scared Lulu to the core and all she wanted to do was stay by her masters and wrap herself around Bailey as best she could. Bailey wanted to play but he realized how upset his little friend was so he lay beside her and let her comfort herself.

"Darn that Amos," Charlie muttered angrily. Bailey looked up and listened to his human friends talking. "He's a miserable jerk and there's no doubt about it."

"He's just that sort of person," Bob said, not looking up from his paper, "We'll just ignore him like we always do and he'll ignore us."

"Oh yeah, like that works," Charlie scoffed, "When was the last time we saw him and he didn't give us some form of grief?"

"Last Wednesday," Bob said, "At the supermarket. He actually got a bottle of olive oil down for me when I couldn't reach."

"Didn't he back into your car?" Charlie asked.

"Oh yeah…" Bob said after a moment's silent thought. "On second thought you're right."

***

The incident at Bob and Charlie's wasn't the first run in between Amos the truck driver and Bailey. It would not be his last. It was a few days later when Bailey decided to go to Old Man Joe's for breakfast. He was full of bacon, just like Bear and they were both toddling along the road, side by side. Joe was a little way behind them, having a small walk into town to collect some supplies. Bailey liked the occasional slow walk he would take with Bear and Joe, both were getting older as the time passed and neither seemed as able to move as quickly as they used to. Bear no longer enjoyed exploring the woods, his bones ached from moving around too much. Instead the big brown dog preferred to lie in the sun and enjoy its warmth. Sometimes Bailey liked to do that too and whenever he was in the mood to lie quietly he would go around to Joe's where the two dogs would lie in the sun and watch the bees buzzing from flower to flower.

Joe decided that he needed some things from town and Bailey decided to tag along. The weather was warm and he realized that he hadn't been to see Barbara for a while. The house where Barbara and Officer Henderson lived was near the town and the three would pass it on their way in. Bailey planned to leave the pair as they passed it so he could revisit his friend while Officer Henderson was out at work.

He would rejoin Bear and Joe when they returned past the house, he could always smell them coming.

For now Joe was tossing a stick around, letting Bailey and Bear race after it. One throw went wide and ended up in the grass on the other side of the road. Bailey was about to run after it when he heard the sound of a truck coming up the road. He recognized the sound and knew that the truck belonged to Angry Amos, the mean truck driver that scared Lulu so much. Bear didn't know and raced across the road to fetch the stick, running as fast as his old joints would take him. He was returning back to his master when the truck appeared and almost hit him. Amos slammed on his brakes at the last moment and the truck screeched to a halt. Amos climbed out, slamming the truck door shut furiously with a tremendous bang.

"What the heck is wrong with you?!" he shouted at Joe, "Don't you keep your dam dogs on leads?"

"What do you know about dogs?" Joe sneered, "You just keep yours tied up outside your house all the time,"

"Because that's what dogs are there for you moron," Amos snarled, "Axel barks at anyone who comes too close and protects my house. He works for me and doesn't get anything otherwise,"

"That's no way to treat a dog!" Joe shouted, "They need to be played with and walked,"

"Well you keep your dog your way and I'll keep my dog my way," Amos snarled, "And you keep your dog on a lead when you're walking him or next time I won't stop you stupid old man,"

The two men continued to exchange angry words but Bailey ran and hid in the bushes. He didn't like Amos at all and although part of him wanted to protect Joe he knew that the old man could protect himself. He didn't simply use his walking stick to help him walk after all. Bailey crouched in the bushes and waited for Amos to leave. Eventually the angry truck driver stomped away after he threw his hands up in the air in frustration. He drove away, once more leaving a cloud of dust and the screech of brakes as he went. Bailey came trotting out of the bushes and returned to Joe's side. The older man was shaking as he put a hand on Bailey's head.

"That's one mean son of a gun right there Buddy," Joe said as he stroked the dog's head, "What does he know about dogs? He leaves his chained up in the yard all the time."

This caught Bailey's interest and he wondered whether this was the chance to make another new friend. But for now his day was planned and he continued on as like nothing happened, following his plans exactly.

***

Bailey almost forgot the possible new friend that lay somewhere on The Hill. It completely slipped his mind until one day he was crossing between Joe's house and Ma and Pops. The truck roared past, heading towards town and carrying the scent of smoke and chewing tobacco. Just smelling that scent reminded Bailey of the dog that lived somewhere nearby, chained up in a yard and he decided that his plans for the day were changed. He left the road that he was following and moved into the forest.

He followed the faint scent of smoke and alcohol that seemed to follow Amos everywhere. The yellow dog moved swiftly through the trees, branches whipping around his head and leaves crunching under his paws. It would soon be winter and already there was a chill in the air. The scent of smoke was getting stronger and eventually Bailey burst out from between the trees into a worn out patch of land where barely anything but grass grew.

This was a place unlike any Bailey ever saw. Everywhere on the Hill was covered in green grass and lush bushes and tall trees. The grass wasn't as green either, more of a dried yellowish brown, like Ma and Pop's field went sometimes when it didn't rain often enough. The smell of smoke and stale alcohol was stronger than ever now and Bailey realized that he was in the right place. He could even see a run-down looking house in the distance and the loud truck parked outside. More importantly he could smell another dog. He barked in excitement and raced over the field towards the house.

He was only a few feet from the house and the fence that surrounded it when the sound of a shotgun boomed out. The ground beside Bailey exploded in a plume of dirt and dust. Bailey yelped and skidded to a halt. He looked around and realized that the shot came from the house that he was heading towards. He looked closer and saw Amos on his porch, waving a shot gun in his direction.

"Get the heck off my property!" Amos shouted, "Get out of here!"

Amos pointed the gun at Bailey but the yellow dog didn't wait to see whether he would shoot. Instead Bailey turned and raced off into the forest. He heard the gun shoot again and felt the bullet slam into the ground somewhere behind him. He yelped and ran faster, bounding between the trees and disappearing between the trees. Today was a day he would not be making a new friend.

***

Bailey didn't give up. He heard the barking of another dog from the house and it didn't sound overly angry or scary. In fact the dog sounded sad and Bailey now wanted more than anything to see this dog and make a new friend. He made so many people and other dogs happy, maybe he could do the same for this dog.

It was a few days before Bailey returned to Amos' house on The Hill. He would have gone back sooner but he was still very, very scared of Amos and his loud gun. He supposed that he should be sure that Amos wasn't there when he went to see Axel. So he found himself sitting in the woods on the very edge of Amos' property. He didn't go any closer, Amos was there, moving around in the yard, shouting and waving his arms around. Bailey was sure that the man spotted him at least once but he hadn't fired his gun at the yellow dog so Bailey supposed that he was safe.

And then he heard it, behind him, the crack of a heavy foot on a twig. Bailey sniffed the air and his mouth dropped open, tongue hanging out as usual. He knew that scent, knew who it belonged to and knew why the owner of the smell was here. Amos called Officer Henderson. Bailey glanced over his shoulder and saw the large man's bulk moving almost silently through the trees, slowly creeping closer and closer. Maybe Bailey wouldn't be able to meet a new friend today but at least he could play with an old one. It had been a while since he and George played the old game of catch the dog.

Bailey sat there, letting the dog catcher get closer and closer. He waited until the man's scent was practically all around him and then he sprang to his feet and ran away. He felt the whoosh of air as the pole swished past him and then he was pelting through the trees. He could hear Officer Henderson swearing and cursing behind him as the man fell over his own legs and got his feet twisted in the loop at the end of his stick. This was almost as much fun as making a new friend.

***

Bailey didn't give up. He kept to the woods, staying well within the shadows. He waited and waited for Amos to leave and go to work or wherever he went in his loud and noisy truck. He made sure that he stayed hidden although once or twice he was sure that Amos spotted him between the tree trunks. One day he was sure of it when he heard the man shouting on the phone.

"What do you mean you can't come and get him?!" Amos shouted, "That's your job isn't it? Catching dogs?!"

Bailey realized that Amos was talking to Officer Henderson and wondered briefly why George didn't just come and play, they always had such a good time together,

"What?!" Amos shouted eventually, "I don't care if you've got a broken leg or a broken head. You're a dog catcher so come and get this dog."

There was another silence.

"'What's it doing?'" Amos seemed to repeat. "Well it's just sitting there, at the edge of my property." A pause, "Well no, it hasn't come on to my property, yet.' Another pause, "So let me get this straight, you can't come and get the dog because it's not actually on my property or causing any problems. Is that right?" A pause, this time longer, "Well what the heck am I supposed to do?!"

Amos threw the phone out of the window and Bailey watched as it smashed on the ground. Apparently George didn't like the angry truck driver any more than Bailey did.

***

He didn't know how much time passed but eventually Amos got into his truck and drove away. The man was carrying a heavy looking bag and he placed a bowl of food and a bowl of water down for the gray dog that was chained up in the yard. The truck rolled away, its tires crunching on the gravel. Once the sounds and smells of the truck faded into the distance Bailey made his move and raced over the field towards what would hopefully be a new friend.

When he reached the fence he wriggled under it and was met by the snapping, snarling face of an angry, bigger dog than he was. Bailey barked in greeting and the other dog seemed to instantly calm down. It looked at Bailey, cocking its head to the side. Bailey did the same thing. This was Axel, he realized, the dog that spent most of his time chained up in the garden. He didn't have friends or people that loved him like Bailey did but Bailey decided that he would change that. He walked past Axel and lay on the ground beside the spot that smelled most strongly of Axel.

Axel watched the yellow dog suspiciously for a few moments before moving to his spot and lying down after he turned around a few times. It was late and he was very tired. Axel settled his head on his paws and found himself drifting into a deep sleep.

***

Amos always knew when the yellow dog was around. Axel always seemed calmer and greeted him with a wagging tail, unlike his usual slow, miserable plod. Amos hated the yellow dog, hated the way that it sat there, at the very edge of his land for days, taunting him. He hated that the yellow dog was coming around and probably drinking all Axel's water and eating all of Axel's food. He tried to complain to Officer Henderson, expecting the dog catcher to do his job and actually catch the dog but the other man never seemed able to help and had a list of excuses that ran a mile long.

Amos knew that the yellow dog was staying over, lying beside Axel in his dog house overnight. Once or twice he arrived back from one of his long distance hauls far earlier than expected and he found the yellow dog curled up with Axel in the little dog house. He hadn't waited, he raced to the house and grabbed the shotgun but by the time he returned to the yard the yellow dog was gone, racing over the field and towards the woods.

Amos also knew that the yellow dog was waiting until he left before it would join Axel on the porch. He caught a glimpse of the creature in his rear view mirror a time or two, it was racing over the field towards Axel and the two leapt into the air in greeting.

"You stupid dingbat," Amos muttered to himself.

That was what Bailey thought he was called at this house eventually. Once or twice, when he was waiting at the edge of Amos' property the man shouted out at him, calling him Dingbat over and over. Bailey didn't know what the name was but knew that in this house, on this little corner of The Hill, his name was apparently Dingbat. Just like with all of his names Bailey liked it

Bailey didn't let Amos scare him away. He was determined to keep Axel company. As soon as he arrived that first night he realized how bored and lonely Axel was. There was no one for Axel to play with, to run around with. There were no ponds or lakes nearby to go swimming and Amos wouldn't even let Axel explore the forests nearby. All that there was in Axel's life was the house that he protected, the dog house that he lived in and the chain that kept him in place. So when Bailey began to visit and they would play a few games Axel was overjoyed.

No longer was he spending night after night after night lying out under the stars, bored as anything. No longer was he disturbed by every single noise and forced to be constantly alert. With Bailey by his side Axel felt at last he could actually sleep and not have to worry about a thing. The nights no longer seemed to stretch for hours. If one or both of the dogs couldn't sleep they could play games and run around until they were both tired enough to sleep. With the company and the fun that the two dogs had together the nights seemed to go by quicker than they ever had. Axel no longer felt there was something big missing from his life. He had a friend, another dog who cared about him now and there was nothing that could take that fact away from him.

***

Amos roared up the road in his truck. He was tired, exhausted even, and all he wanted to do was lie on his bed and pass out for a few hours. He wondered why he kept doing what he did, driving the big rigs around the state and across the country. They took him away for days at a time and the bed in the cabin was not nearly as comfortable as it once was. Then again the money was good and he got a fair amount of time off between jobs. Amos realized that maybe it was about time that he spent some of the money that he was earning on a new bed. It was just sitting in his savings account after all.

When he pulled up to his house he immediately knew that there was something wrong. That blasted Dingbat was lying on his porch, right next to Axel. In fact the two stupid dogs were curled up together. Amos grumbled to himself and climbed down from his truck. Before he shut the door he reached for the baseball bat he kept behind the driver's seat. He jumped down to the ground and was a little surprised when Dingbat and Axel only looked up briefly before resting their heads on their paws again.

There was definitely something wrong. Amos knew that Dingbat stayed with Axel some nights, there was no way of ignoring that fact. His dog changed so much since Dingbat first started appearing on his land. But usually the yellow dog was gone by the time that Amos returned from his travels. Occasionally he even saw the dog running off into the woods as he drove up the driveway. Today Dingbat was just lying there, panting, as if he no longer cared what happened.

Amos walked closer, slowly. Something made the hair on the back of his neck stand on end. He opened the gate to his yard and stepped on to the gravel. But instead of the usual satisfying crunch that came from beneath his boots today he only heard a wet sloppy sound, more like when it rained. Amos looked down and almost dropped his bat. He looked around the yard and took in the scene of devastation that surrounded him.

There was blood everywhere, pooling wherever it could, splattered across the usually white and gray gravel. Tufts of hair littered the ground, some with small chunks of flesh still attached. Amos knelt down and picked up some of the fur, rubbing it between his fingers. It was a brownish yellow color that didn't match either of the coats of the two dogs in front of him. It was coarse and smelled foul. Amos rose to his full height and slowly walked around the yard.

He found a hole in the fence around his property, tufts of fur stuck to the pointed edges that were still dripping a little blood although most of it was dry. There were paw prints around the hole and some in the pools of blood. Some clearly belonged to Dingbat, they were just the right size and the dog's paws were covered in blood. But some were bigger, unlike any dog paw prints he had ever seen. Then Amos looked closer and realized that some of the fur littering the yard was gray like Axel's and some was a bright yellow, like Dingbat's. He looked closer at the prints and realized that he knew what they belonged to.

"Did you chase off a coyote?" he asked Dingbat.

The dog just looked at him and it was then that Amos realized that there was blood all over the yellow dog. It looked tired and there were a few shallow bite marks on his flanks. Beside Dingbat Axel looked equally tired. Amos looked around the yard closely and saw that there was more blood by the dog house than there was anywhere else. The fur that littered the ground there was in clumps, some still oozing a little blood onto the earth. Finally Amos realized that sometime in the night a coyote must have come sniffing around and was prepared to attack his chained up dog. Dingbat must have chased the coyote off, giving as good as he got to keep Axel safe. Amos couldn't understand why, the other dog could just have run away and escaped the coyote. Then he realized that with the chain Axel couldn't have gotten away. If it were not for Dingbat Axel would have been dead and Amos' property would probably have been ruined by a wild animal searching for food. Amos dropped his bat to the ground.

***

After that Amos didn't have the heart to level his gun at Dingbat any more. That wasn't to say that he made a new best friend. Whenever he saw the yellow dog on his property he would shout and yell until Dingbat turned and ran back the way he came. But he didn't get out the shotgun or call Officer Henderson any more. As more time passed and Axel's wounds began to heal Amos also found himself being kinder to the dog. Whenever he returned from a long trip he would pat the dog on the head and get him some food and water, no matter how tired Amos was himself. He lengthened the chain too, giving the dog more room to run and play with. From time to time, when the weather was particularly bad Amos began to let Axel inside his house, to lie on the kitchen floor. He still wasn't the champion of all things small and furry but Amos found himself being kinder to the animals around it and, although he didn't admit it, he was actually growing fonder and fonder of Axel with each day.

Bailey continued to visit Axel, spending time with his friend. He was no longer scared of Amos but knew that the man didn't really like him that much. He made sure to avoid him as best he could, simply to keep the peace. It was a bit like with Shadow all over again except Amos no longer threatened to hurt him anymore. Instead the man just made sure that Bailey knew that he wasn't welcome when Amos was around. Bailey could live with that. He had many friends who liked to have him around all the time; one that didn't wouldn't make a difference to him.

"Yellow Dog in his younger days."

"Yellow Dog in the pond"

"Older Yellow Dog"

"One of the roads Yellow Dog traveled"

"A view from one of the roads Yellow Dog traveled daily"

"Yellow Dog in the yard"

"A happy Yellow Dog"

"Yellow Dog with one of the Shepherds"

"Another road traveled by Yellow Dog"

"The woods traveled by Yellow Dog"

"The yard where the Shepherds live"

"Yellow Dog playing with one of the Shepherds"

"The Shepherds"

"One of the Shepherds chasing Yellow Dog"

"Yellow Dog enjoying the snow"

Chapter 9

A Lost Boy

Cody kicked at the ground, hands in his pockets and head hanging low. He was pacing up and down outside his house, waiting for his grandparents to finish talking to the shrink. He wondered what drugs they'd put him on this time, what pills they'd force him to swallow in the attempt to make him normal. Why didn't they get that he wasn't normal. He never would be. All the kids at school knew he was weird, a loner, a little frightened and always sad. At one time they tried to talk to him, tried to get him to join in with their games. But eventually, after he refused time after time they finally realized that they were wasting their breath. Now they played their games while Cody sat and watched from the sidelines. Occasionally he wished that they would invite him to play again but the feeling would soon pass and Cody would go back to staring at the ground and trying to fight back the tears.

He could feel his eyes burning already, just thinking about it all. He just never fit in, he hadn't for years. He supposed it was all because his parents died when he was three. He knew other students at school who were raised by other family members but they knew their parents and saw them regularly. He was the only one who didn't. That was what marked him as different in their eyes. He was different in his own mind too. He just didn't know who his parents were or where he came from. He heard stories of course, his grandparents made sure that he knew who his parents were. But that was all they were, stories. He never really knew them, he never knew how they would respond to his stories of his days at school, and he didn't know what advice they would give him with his problems.

As he passed up and down the garden he wondered whether he would fit in if he had a mother. He couldn't help but ask himself whether he would be a different person if he had a mother to give him hugs and tuck him into bed or a father who would take him fishing. He knew Lilly and Grant tried, they really did, but they were old and couldn't get around as much as they used to. Their ideas of fun and a good childhood were a little different to his. They were from a different era, it wasn't their fault. But still it hurt.

"Cody?" he heard Grandma Lilly shouting from the front step. "Cody where are you?"

He knew she was panicking. And he knew it was his own fault.

"I'm over here," he called.

Grandma Lilly came around the side of the house just as Cody settled himself on the swing. He swung himself on it listlessly, eyes fixed down on the ground.

"Cody…" Grandma said quietly, her voice full of concern. "Cody, Doctor Phillip suggested we put you on a new medication,"

"Not another one," he said with a grumpy sigh. "I hate those things. They make me feel all foggy."

"I know sweetheart," Lilly said as she put her hand on the back of Cody's head, "But it's for your own good. Without them it just gets too much and I can't bear another repeat of November."

"Grandma…" Cody said listlessly. "I…"

Cody was lost for words. He knew he needed something to help him. He already tried to take his own life once in the past year. It scared him just as much as it scared his grandparents. He still couldn't understand why he did it. All he knew was that the sadness and the pain had just gotten to be too much. As soon as he was found and came around in the hospital he couldn't believe what he tried to do. That was when the drugs and the therapy began. He did admit that he felt a little better for a while but he still didn't feel normal and the drugs made him feel really odd.

"I love you Cody," Lilly said eventually, "You know that don't you?"

"Of course," Cody said, smiling weakly at his grandma, "I love you too."

Grandma Lilly pulled Cody into a deep hug and kissed his head. Cody hugged her back and breathed in the scent that always comforted him. He just wanted to be normal.

***

Bailey saw that it was a beautiful day as he walked away from Joe's house. He ate his breakfast already, a large selection of bacon already and a cookie was his early morning snack. He stayed the night at Marianne's getting the feeling that she needed him that night. She gave him a cookie, the usual peanut butter, and ate it and played with her little dogs before he walked to Joe's. He hadn't been there in a while and missed seeing Bear. Bear missed him too. Now his tummy was full and the day was sunny and the wind was blowing lightly through his fur. As he walked down the road he wondered where he would go today.

He wanted to make a new friend. Axel was so much happier now that he started visiting him but Amos was at home so he couldn't visit. All of his other friends were once more busy or away from The Hill so Bailey just didn't know where to go. Then, as he walked along the road he spotted somewhere that he hadn't been before. It was a little road, narrow and mostly dirt. It was covered by trees, creating a tunnel of green. The sunlight dappled the ground in patterns. Bailey decided that he wanted to see what was at the end of the tunnel. So he left the road and headed up that dark path.

***

Cody was walking around the garden, waving a stick back and forth. He was alone, completely this time. His grandparents headed into town and he made sure that they thought he was completely ok. He couldn't take it anymore, he was tired of feeling so yucky all the time. He was only 12 years old and already he felt about 30. It was just too much emotion to handle and the thought of an entire lifetime feeling as bad as he did right now just made him feel worse. He knew that his sadness would get stronger and more overwhelming as he got older, Grandpa Grant had already had the talk about puberty and the way that hormones made people's emotions go all crazy. Cody didn't want to go through that, he knew that he wouldn't be able to cope. Finally, his grandparents would not be around forever, then what would happen to him?

He checked his watch and saw that his grandparents were gone for over half an hour now. They would be in town for at least two hours and it would take them just over half an hour to get back. He was going to make sure that there were no mistakes this time, that he wasn't found and saved. So he needed to do it now, within the next few minutes. Cody pulled the shed key out of his pocket and moved around the back of the house.

***

Bailey saw the boy in the garden. He saw the way that the boy's shoulders were slumped, the way he was kicking the ground and waving a stick around. He didn't seem to care, about anything. Bailey recognized those movements, they had the same sadness to them that Marianne's used to, when he had first come to visit. When the boy disappeared around the side of the house, pulling something shiny from his pocket a bad feeling settled in Bailey's belly and he raced through the garden and around to the back of the house. The boy was going towards the shed. Bailey didn't like the smell of the shed, there were things in there that made his nose twitch and made him want to sneeze. The boy shouldn't go in the shed. Bailey sat down, at the corner of the house and barked sharply.

***

At first Cody didn't know where the barking was coming from. There were no dogs nearby, he knew that much. He stopped and looked around the woods behind his grandparent's house. There was nothing moving. Then the bark came again and he realized that it was coming from behind him. Slowly he turned around, nervous about what kind of dog might be barking at him. His heart was pounding.

"Oh..." he said.

It was a yellow dog, just sitting by the corner of the house. It was looking right at him, head cocked to one side and tail wagging.

"Hello." Cody said.

The dog barked again, standing up. It slowly trotted towards him, tongue hanging out and tail wagging the entire time. Cody took a few hesitant steps towards it and then grew a little bolder. He held out a hand, trembling slightly. The dog just raised its head, sniffed it and then licked his hand with a wet, warm, soft tongue. It tickled.

"Hey you," Cody said softly. "Where'd you come from?"

He knelt beside the dog and searched its soft yellow fur for a collar or a tag. There was nothing there. The dog seemed to think he was playing and began to lick at Cody's face. It tickled just as much and Cody soon found himself laughing and falling to the ground. His arms were wrapped around the dog's neck, fingers digging into the fur and scratching wildly. The dog's tail wagged madly to and fro and it whined in happiness. The boy and the dog wrestled for a while, laughing and barking. Eventually Cody grew tired and collapsed on his back, staring up at the sky. The dog lay beside him, head resting on Cody's chest. Cody sighed and played with the dog's ears. The dog sighed too and groaned with happiness. The entire time the yellow dog's tail was wagging in the dirt.

"You're a good boy," Cody said eventually, "I like you."

The yellow dog shoved his nose against Cody's hand, demanding that the scratches to his ears be continued. Cody laughed and continued to do as the dog wanted. He looked up at the sky, smiling broadly. For the first time in his life he felt normal, almost happy. Perhaps there was hope for him yet.

***

When Lilly and Grant returned to the house they were instantly worried. The front door was wide open and there was no sign of Cody in the front of the house. Lilly's heart was pounding as she leapt out of the car before it stopped and raced towards the house. She knew there was something wrong with Cody. He tried to hide it but she knew that he was still so sad. His behavior reminded her of the days before he tried to kill himself, the worst time of her life. She already lost her daughter, she couldn't lose her grandson too. Her heart raced as she ran around the side of the house. She slowed as she came to the corner that led to the back. She could hear laughing, something that she hadn't heard in a long time. Footsteps came from behind her and she felt her husband's hand on the small of her back.

"Where is he?" Grant asked quietly. "Is that him?"

"I think so," she said just as quietly, "What's he doing?"

The couple crept around the side of the house and froze. Cody was wrestling on the ground with a yellow dog. For a moment Lilly was terrified, thinking that her beloved grandson was being attacked. But then the dog broke away, bouncing around the garden and Cody knelt there, laughing and trying to follow the dog while still staying on his knees. She hadn't seen him so happy in such a long time. There was color in his cheeks and a brightness to his eyes that she didn't even realized was missing. She sobbed quietly.

It wasn't quietly enough. Cody froze, smile plastered on his face and looked towards the house. He slowly climbed to his feet, still smiling and laughing as the yellow dog raced up to him and tried to knock him over again.

"Stop that silly," he eventually managed to say through his giggles, "I'm trying to say hello to grandma and grandpa."

He walked over to his grandma and gave her a huge hug. Lilly was frozen for a moment. Cody never hugged her first, she always hugged him first. Now here he was, wrapping his arms around her and squeezing tightly. She eventually wrapped her arms around her grandson and hugged him back.

"Who's this fellow?" Grant asked.

He knelt down to look at the yellow dog who instantly began licking at his face and wagging his tail.

"He seems friendly," Grant said once he managed to get the dog away from his face. It was now sitting beside him, letting him stroke its head, "Where'd he come from?"

"I don't know," Cody said with a shrug, "I just turned around and he was there."

"What have I told you about strange dogs," Lilly scolded.

"He's friendly Grandma," Cody whined, sounding like the 12 year old boy that he was at last, "I didn't rush to him, I let him come to me, just like you taught me. I could have got to the house if he was dangerous,"

"If he was dangerous Officer Henderson would have caught him by now," Grant said. He rubbed roughly at the dog's chest and spoke to the yellow dog like a small child, "Wouldn't he? He'd have come and got you. You're not dangerous are you boy? Are you? You're just a happy guy."

The yellow dog seemed to love the attention and panted in happiness. Cody giggled and raced off across the garden.

"Come on Happy," he called, "Let's go play."

The yellow dog barked and raced off after the young boy. Cody's laughter filled the air. Grant climbed to his feet, groaning as his knees cracked. He threw an arm around Lilly's slim shoulders and held her close.

"What was he doing outside?" she asked quietly,

"I don't want to know," Grant said firmly, "It couldn't have been for anything good. I spotted the shed key in his pocket,"

"Oh my goodness!" Lilly gasped, "All the chemicals in there. Do you think he was…"

"I don't want to think about what he was going to do," Grant said firmly, "The fact is he didn't and we have that dog to thank for that."

"He came just at the right time," Lilly said quietly, squeezing her husband's hand, "I've never seen Cody so happy,"

"It's like he was sent here to cheer Cody up," Grant agreed. "Sent at just the right time and to just the right place."

"Do you think it was Suzanne?" Lilly asked quietly.

"Well if it was any one sending that dog it would be her," Grant said, "Whatever she sent him for he's certainly helping our boy. We should give thanks for that."

"Yes," Lilly said, "And we should buy him some nice treats too,"

"I'll go back into town," Grant said with a sigh.

Lily laughed as her husband headed back around the front of the house. She glanced over her shoulder and saw the boy and the dog playing together. She closed her eyes with a smile and sent a silent prayer of thanks to her daughter, wherever she was.

***

Bailey loved visiting Cody, almost the most out of all of his friends. He was like a dog in human form in Bailey's mind. He was full of energy and always so happy to see Bailey. Cody had so much energy and would happily explore for hours. Together they wandered the woods, Cody would climb trees and throw sticks down for Bailey to chase after. Bailey, or Happy as Cody called him, would sniff out rabbit holes and Cody would lay rough traps. Of course the traps never really caught anything but they would sit nearby, watching the rabbit holes. Cody would talk to Happy about everything and anything that came to mind. Happy loved it, loved listening to all the stories Cody would tell him. He spoke of a world beyond the Hill, full of people that Happy wanted to meet and make his friends. He knew he never would but still he liked to imagine it.

Sometimes, when Cody was talking, his voice would be so full of sadness that Happy would curl up next to him, put his head on Cody's knees and whine gently to let the boy know he wasn't alone any more. A time or two Cody ended up wrapping his arms around Happy and crying into the dog's fur, letting out all of the anger and the hurt that filled him up. It was at those times that Happy really wished he had arms that he could wrap around the boy. As it was all he could do was wait until Cody stopped crying and then lick the salty tears from his face. The tears and sadness would soon be replaced by laughter and smiles. Happy felt happy that he was helping someone who had once been so sad. Happy liked to do that, he did it for so many other people and now he was doing it for someone who quite possibly needed it the most.

Best of all Cody knew all of the secret paths and roads that Happy never saw before. No one walked along them, they were old dirt tracks slowly being overgrown with plants and bushes. Cody would ride his bike down those tracks, going as fast as he could. Happy would run alongside, going just as fast. Sometimes he would pull ahead and other times Cody would ride ahead, disappearing around a corner before Happy could keep up. Whenever Happy went around and reached the corner there was Cody, always waiting for him.

They would go fishing together, down at the old creek that ran through the woods and towards the town. Happy would lie on the bank, enjoying the sunshine and occasionally jumping into the water to cool off. Cody would sit on the bank, patiently fishing. He liked to lean on Happy's body, listening to the dog's heart beat and knowing that even though he might be alone he wasn't completely alone and there was someone who loved him, unconditionally. Happy's favorite thing about those days was the lunches that Lilly always packed for Cody. There was always too much. She made sure that Happy could have a lunch too and Cody would toss pieces of the sandwich into the meadow by the creek and Happy would sniff them out. There was almost always a nice juicy bone, the big leg bone of a cow or some other animal, sawed down to fit and Happy would sit there, gnawing at it while Cody fished.

They would even go out on the canoe together. Cody would row hard, sending the little boat zooming across the small lake and Happy would stand at the bow, enjoying the surf in his face. Cody would fish while Happy stared into the water or they would just sit there, enjoying the sun and watching the sky go around and around as the canoe spun on the surface of the water. Cody loved all of their trips, just as much as Happy. He no longer felt he was hovering on the brink of tears all of the time. He no longer found himself wishing for a life that he never had. He still missed his parents but the pain was lessened; no longer as sharp or hurtful as it once was. Happy made the sadness, the anger, and the loneliness go away. Cody had a friend that none of the other children at school had. A friend that wouldn't be mean to him or make fun of him. A friend that always seemed to know when he was needed and never argued with him. Happy was a friend that knew sometimes Cody got sad and it wouldn't make him angry or irritated. The yellow dog would just sit there, being there and letting Cody know, in his doggy way, that the boy wasn't alone.

"I love you Happy," Cody said quietly one afternoon in the canoe.

Happy couldn't speak but he told Cody that he loved him too by licking the boy's cheek gently, just once, and then resting his head back on his paws.

"You're the best," Cody said.

He shifted suddenly, swatting at a bee that was buzzing around his head. The sudden movement rocked the canoe and there was a loud splash. Cody sat up, wiggling around until he was settled securely in the canoe. He looked over the edge and saw one of the oars drifting across the lake's surface, away from them.

"Oh no!" Cody cried. Happy whined and Cody pointed at the oar, "We can't get back to the shore without it. It's getting away."

Happy stood on the edge of the canoe and barked at the oar, demanding that it come back immediately. He made the boat rock for a moment and Cody cried out, grabbing the sides of the canoe to steady it. When the oar didn't come back Happy looked at Cody and whined.

"I know Happy," Cody said, "I can't go and get it, Grandma Lilly'll kill me if I get my clothes wet again."

Happy looked from Cody and to the oar and back again. Then without a moment's hesitation he leapt into the lake with a loud splash, sending water flying everywhere. Cody laughed, shielding himself for a moment. He looked out over the lake and saw Happy swimming towards the oar, bound and determined to reach it. The dog's head bobbed up and down in the water as he paddled, a bright splash of yellow on the dull brown of the lake. Eventually Happy reached the oar, took it in his mouth and dragged it back to Cody who happily took it from the dog's mouth. Happy couldn't get back into the canoe, the angle was too awkward and Cody wasn't strong enough to pick him up and lift him into their small boat.

"Swim to the shore Boy!" Cody called, pointing to the nearby shore. "Go on, swim!"

Happy swam through the water, tail wagging and splashing around. Cody followed slowly behind in the canoe.

***

Happy liked Cody's grandparents, Lilly and Grant, just as much as he loved Cody. They always saw him coming and greeted him with smiles and happiness. Grant would have a ball to throw around the garden when it was sunny but Cody was too tired to explore far. Sometimes, when Cody was really sad and wanted to be left alone, Grant would play fetch with Happy in the garden, throwing the ball around and letting the yellow dog race to go and get it. Now and then he would be gardening, tending the flowers and pulling up the weeds. Cody would help him, liking to learn something new, especially about somewhere that he so loved. Happy would lie nearby and when they needed something that was outside of their reach he would run and get it for them, carrying it to their reaching hands in his mouth. They would always give him a rub and a tickle on the tummy when he did that.

Happy loved Lilly too. She was soft and warm and would always have a treat for him to nibble on. As soon as he appeared at whichever door was closest to Cody she would bring out a bowl of water so he could quench his thirst. It was hard work after all, visiting so many friends all over the Hill. Then she would hold out her hand with a small piece of meat or a special chewy dog bone for him to chomp on before Cody and he could go on their adventures. If it was raining she would open the door straight away and wrap Happy in a towel to dry him off, rubbing his fur all over.

On those days she would encourage the two to stay in the kitchen, Cody to help her bake or cook and Happy to eat anything that they dropped on the floor. She pretended to disapprove of course but Happy knew she was just joking. She never once used the wooden spoon that she waved at him.

Happy was a clever dog too and Cody knew it. On the rainy days when Cody didn't want to go outside into the cold and wet the boy and the dog would disappear into Cody's room. Inside, in their secret little hideaway Cody would do his best to teach Happy all sorts of tricks. Some Happy already knew, having been taught them already. Others were completely new to him and it seemed that Cody got them from moving pictures on a small box in his room. The boy liked to show Happy the moving pictures and then he would try to teach Happy the tricks that he had just seen. As clever as Happy was it was still hard for him to learn those tricks, especially some of the harder ones. He tried and tried and the two would spend the entire day practicing until Happy realized that it was time for him to go home or visit another friend.

When Happy learned enough new tricks he would put on a show for Lilly and Grant. Cody would direct him and Happy would try his hardest to get the tricks that he learned right. It never really mattered, if the tricks were done right or wrong. Lilly and Grant always laughed and applauded, no matter what happened and at the end of the trick show they would pull Cody on to the sofa and into a hug. Happy didn't like being left out of those hugs and he would jump up, on to their knees, lying across everyone. That made everyone laugh so hard and they would all hug him and kiss him too.

He would give just as many kisses back, wet slobbering dog kisses with his big pink tongue. They were the same kisses that he gave when it was time to go home to Ben and Mark.

Cody didn't like Happy leaving to go somewhere else of course, Happy could smell it all over the young boy. But Cody also knew that Happy wasn't really his dog. He knew that the dog had another family that loved him as much as Cody did and would probably get very upset if they didn't get him back. Of course their parting was made easier by the fact that Cody knew that Happy would always come back to him, no matter what. He was glad that he had Happy in his life at all. The dog made everything seem a little better and life that much easier to handle. Things no longer seemed as dark or as bleak as they once did and Cody knew that no matter how bad he might feel, how bad things could get for him, Happy would always be there to make things better in his own, small doggy way.

Chapter 10

The Hunter

Bailey was having the time of his life. Bear seemed to have found a new lease of life and was happy to go adventuring with him all the time again. Old Man Joe said it was because the vet finally managed to figure out why he was so bloated all the time and now it was fixed Bear could run around all he wanted because he had so much more energy. Bailey didn't really care what was wrong with Bear but was just happy that he was better and could returning to doing what they used to do. Cody was back at school for the autumn and without his friend to keep him company during the day Bailey was wondering what to do with himself. He really enjoyed wandering around the woods with Cody, even if the human boy couldn't run as fast or as far as Bailey could. Bailey loved him anyway. But now he was away every day they couldn't go exploring like they did in the summer. And then Bear got better.

Bailey trotted through the woods towards Joe's house. He could smell people in the woods, hear them crashing around through the undergrowth. There was the smell of gunpowder in the air, faint but unmistakable. It smelled like Mark's garden did when he was having one of his parties and started shooting his guns off. It sounded like it too. Every now and then Bailey would hear the faint sound of a shot, far off in the distance. Once or twice it was much closer. He didn't like the sound, it was too unpredictable and he never knew when it was coming. When the shots were from nearby they hurt his ears too a little.

This wasn't a new thing, it happened before, at least once a year when the leaves started to turn orange. But Bailey was always close to home, wandering around Ma and Pop's farm or playing with Lulu in the garden. He hadn't wanted to bother Joe who tended to be busy shoring up his cabin for winter when the guns came. And Bear was too tired and sore to go exploring. With Bear so much better, Bailey wanted to do what they used to do and he was determined that no loud gunshots would scare him off.

***

"Hey Buddy!" Joe cried as soon as Bailey stepped out of the woods, "You're just in time for breakfast."

Bailey raced across the garden and up the stairs, bounding up all three steps and settling himself on the porch in one move. Bear already buried his face in his bowl, gobbling down slices of bacon like the hungry bear that was his namesake.

"I was wondering how long it would take you to get here," Joe said with a smile.

He placed Buddy's bowl on the porch and shoveled in some bacon. As Buddy ducked his head to start eating Joe scratched behind his ears and then left him to eat. Buddy's tail wagged hard as he slowly ate his way through the bacon breakfast. He liked to take it slow, savoring the taste of the salty meat. Even when he was really hungry Buddy always ate his bacon one strip at a time, not like Bear at all. Bear already finished his bowl of bacon and came over to sniff at Buddy's bowl. But Buddy was having none of it and growled softly, warning his friend away. Bear stopped where he was for a moment before he slowly backed away. Buddy wasn't satisfied that his breakfast was safe and shifted his body around until he lay between Bear and the bowl of bacon.

"Bear, you leave Buddy alone," Joe said as he came out of the cabin, "You've had your breakfast, let him have his."

Bear whined slightly, looking up at Joe with wide brown eyes. Joe smiled and sat down, gently pushing Bear's face away when he came to put his head on Joe's knee. Joe had bacon of his own and was eating it with some scrambled eggs.

"Get out of here," Joe said with a laugh, "The vet said you're not allowed as much as I was giving you. If you're still hungry go and eat some of your own food. The food for dogs, not people food,"

Bear glanced at the bowl of dried dog food that Joe put out. It was piled high with small pellets of different shapes and colors. It didn't smell nearly as good as the bacon that Joe was eating smelled. Bear sneezed at the bowl and turned back to stare at his master. Then Buddy barked, his bacon now all eaten and in his stomach. Bear glanced at his friend before turning back to Joe and whining softly.

"Go on," Joe said, pointing towards the woods with his fork, "Get out of here and have some fun."

Bear rocked in place for a few moments. Joe grumbled and gently nudged him with his foot.

"Get!" Joe called. "Go explore or whatever it is you do."

Buddy barked and Bear finally got to his paws. He raced after Buddy who took off towards the tree. Joe watched them go with a smile on his face. Then he returned to his breakfast and picked up the newspaper, reading as he ate. The sudden sound of a gunshot made him jump, almost making him knock over his coffee. He looked around, hearing more of the gunshot and cursed. He forgot all about hunting season and now his dogs were wandering around the woods, woods which were full of hunters ready to shoot anything that moved.

"Gosh darnit!" Joe muttered.

He raced into his house, carrying his dishes with him and tossing them in his sink. He then started rummaging through the various containers that housed his things, searching for something that was eluding him.

***

Bear really didn't like the sound of the gunshots, Buddy could tell. Every time one came the big brown dog would whimper and cringe, huddling close to the ground trying to hide from it. Buddy was trying to lead his friend away from the gunshots and whoever was setting them off. He'd been trying all morning in fact but the going was slow, made even slower by Bear stopping completely every time the shots rang out. Buddy began to wonder whether it may have been better to stay on Joe's property, maybe playing in the meadow with the bees. Every time that he thought he escaped the gunshots they would come again from a different direction. The entire woods were filled with gun happy people who didn't seem to care for anything else that might make the trees their home. Buddy was getting fed up and seriously considered taking Bear back and going to see Marianne instead.

***

Alfie sat hidden among the trees. He shifted in his chair slightly, trying to ease his aching muscles. The chair was a simple fold up one that gave little actual support. It creaked every time that he moved and he found himself wincing each time the creaking came. Sometimes it was loud and sometimes it was so quiet that he almost missed the sound all together. But the sound did come and it was annoying. Alfie considered just giving up on the chair and crouching in the hide instead.

He shifted again and glanced down the barrel of his hunting rifle. There wasn't a thing moving in the clearing that he was facing. He'd seen a few deer visiting throughout the day but each time he moved, something creaked startling the deer and sending them running into the undergrowth. It didn't help that the sounds of rifles and shot guns were ringing out all over The Hill. If the animals couldn't hear those then there was no point hunting them.

"Why didn't I come during the week?" he muttered to himself.

There wasn't a single piece of movement in the clearing and Alfie asked himself the same question again. He had a full time job, sure, but he was owed vacation time. Coming during the week would have meant less other hunters around and a better chance of bagging a deer or something. It was just too noisy now, at the weekend, and the whole forest probably stank of humans. He knew that the hide definitely did.

Something moved in the clearing, right at the edge, between all of the leaves that draped down from the trees and bushes. Alfie leveled his rifle at the movement and rest his finger on the trigger. He was ready to squeeze it and maybe take out a deer or something. If it were a bear that would be even better. The leaves parted slowly and something brown slowly stepped into the clearing.

"Darn it man I could have shot you!" Alfie shouted.

He lowered his weapon, casually tossing it to one sound in frustration. He climbed down from the hide and advanced on the old man who came into the clearing.

"Sorry," the old man said, not even looking at the hunter.

"Don't you know you're supposed to wear one of these when you're out in the forest at this time of year?" Alfie asked loudly, tugging at his own florescent jacket. "You could get shot by anyone who mistakes you for an animal."

"That's why I'm here," Joe said absently.

He wasn't paying attention to the hunter who was now looking very confused. Instead he was slowly turning in a circle, whistling through his teeth and looking around. On Joe the expression looked more like he was sucking a lemon.

"You came here to get shot?" Alfie asked in disbelief. "Aren't there easier ways to kill yourself?"

"I didn't come here to get shot you imbecile," Joe snapped, "I came here to stop my dogs from getting shot."

Joe held up a hand that was clutching two orange vests. He waved them in the hunter's face.

"What the hell were you thinking?" Alfie asked in disbelief, "You just let your dogs run around the woods in hunting season without even giving them some protection? What is wrong with you?"

"Nothing," Joe snapped, "I'm just old is all. I don't remember stuff like I used to. I forgot it was even close to hunting season until I heard the gunshots."

"What do they look like?" Alfie asked with a sigh as he reached for his radio, "I can put out an alert for you,"

"One's big and brown," Joe said quickly, "The other one is all yellow, a Labrador,"

"And the brown one's breed?" Alfie asked as he twisted the knob to get the right channel.

"He's a mutt," Joe said, "He's got a bit of everything in him. But he's big and fluffy and looks a little bit like a bear,"

"Well that's helpful," Alfie said sarcastically. He raised the radio to his mouth, "Attention all hunters, attention all hunters, this is Alfie in Sector Four. Be on the look out for two dogs, one brown and built like a bear, the other a yellow Lab. I repeat, be on the look out for two dogs. They have no vests on and they're running around the woods."

The radio quickly squawked out a bunch of varying replies and Alfie looked at Joe.

"There you go," Alfie said, "People will be keeping an eye out for them. If you're going to keep looking you're going to need a visibility vest. The last thing we need is some guy getting shot looking for his dogs."

Joe managed to eventually mumble out that he didn't have a vest. Alfie wasn't listening. He turned to his pack and was digging through. Eventually he pulled out a slightly tattered looking day glow orange vest and handed it to Joe.

"Here," he said, "Put this on and try to stick to the main paths."

Joe thanked the hunter and pulled on the vest. By the time that the old man looked up Alfie disappeared back into his hide and Joe was all alone in the clearing. He tucked the vests for the dogs into his pockets and retraced his steps, trying to find the path through the woods that he wandered away from.

***

Buddy and Bear were having the time of their lives. Bear eventually got used to the sounds of the gunshots and now they were racing around the woods, trying to find the sources of the sounds. Buddy wanted to make some new friends and today the wood was full of them. There would be no better time than today to spend the entire day meeting new and interesting people. Neither dog had any idea of the danger that they were in. Buddy had never actually seen the guns that Mark shot hit anything, he didn't know the damage that a bullet could do. He didn't even know that the guns actually fired things, he just saw them as black sticks that made loud noises and a bad smell.

They bounced through the woods without a care in the world. They could smell the deer that were around, tracking their scent trails with their keen noses. They sniffed out rabbit holes and squirrel tracks. The dogs chased anything that they could spot, making sure not to bark and give themselves away. The two dogs were on the trail of a great buck with wide antlers that they were following for half an hour, although neither one could tell the time.

The buck was leading them on a merry chase through the trees and Buddy was sure that it was playing with them. Every time that it seemed to pull away from them and disappear they would quickly find it again, standing waiting for them. They would give chase as soon as they spotted it and the buck would bound away again. They were having the time of their lives and exploring unknown parts of the forest.

When Bear stopped to catch his breath and cool off for a while Buddy started to realize that there was something different about the woods today, something that didn't belong other than the sound of the guns firing. Both dogs sat side by side panting, their tails wagging and smiles on their doggy faces. Buddy sniffed the air and smelled something unusual. It was metallic, musky and salty all at the same time. It smelled like Joe's bacon before he cooked it, like the horses when they caught their flesh on sharp pieces of the fence, like Marianne's fingers when she used a knife to cook and cried out. Flashes of red came into Buddy's mind and he realized that what he was smelling was blood.

He couldn't understand why there was blood in the forest. There was the occasional whiff of it here and there, the natural order of things meaning that something was hurt or killed from time to time. But the smell never lingered except for in the place where it happened. And even then the scent was never this strong, it didn't fill the place beneath the trees like it did now. Buddy whined quietly and nudged Bear with his nose. The brown dog picked up on the scent too after he noticed what Buddy was doing. He didn't like it either. The smell was too strong and it was coming from everywhere. Something was very wrong in their woods and they had to get out.

Together the two dogs took off, racing one behind the other as they weaved their way through the trees. They had to get to the road, out of the woods, and away from the smell of death that was filling the forest.

***

Elliot set his sights on the yearling in front of him. It was a male deer, barely old enough to be growing antlers. But they were there, tiny little things on top of its delicate head. The deer was picking at fresh shoots on the ground, daintily nibbling at the blade of grass and flowers. Now and then it looked up, its ears flicking around, back and forth and it looked around. He almost felt guilty for planning on shooting the deer but at the same time it was a chance that couldn't be missed. It was Elliot's first solo hunt. Usually he went with a few of his brothers and they sat in the hide, taking it in turns to watch for deer or rabbits.

Now he was allowed out on his own. He'd spent a lot of the day searching for the perfect hide, well away from the other hunters that he knew were out there. And then he proceeded to settle himself down and keep an eye out for his prey. The deer was there, waiting for him to squeeze the trigger. But he couldn't yet, there was no clear shot and if he were to fire now the only thing that he would manage would be to wound the animal, not kill it.

That was what his dad and brothers taught him. He wanted to get a clean shot and kill the creature out right.

Anything else was just cruel and unnecessary. His dad sometimes scolded him when he first started out and messed up a shot. There were deer and rabbits that were injured by his wild shots, some only scratched while others were left with terrible wounds that slowed them down, left them bleeding and in pain. His dad made him track those ones and put them out of them out of their misery himself.

It was a task he hated and seeing the pain and the suffering that his wild shots created in those poor animals meant that it wasn't long before he started to be much more careful with his shots. Besides, a clean shot left a better pelt and the meat was cleaner too. So now Elliot sat waiting for the deer to move more fully out from behind the tree so he could finally squeeze the trigger and get his bullet right into the heart.

The dear looked up again and Elliot held his breath for a moment. Every muscle in his body was tense, tight, waiting to see what the buck would do. It was looking towards the edge of the clearing, a little to one side of where Elliot was hiding. There was something rustling in the undergrowth. The deer could hear it. Its ears were pointed right towards the sound, not flicking around like they were before. Elliot fought the temptation to turn around and see what was making the sound, he kept his eyes fixed on the buck. It took a couple of steps away from the tree, finally coming out.

Elliot hissed quietly and shifted his rifle into a better position. His finger slowly squeezed at the trigger like he was taught. Then the deer took a few more steps forward. Elliot adjusted his aim and squeezed. The gun went off, a small cloud of gunpowder erupting from the end. Elliot imagined that he could see the bullet sweeping through the air, right towards the buck's chest. But the buck moved, twisting back on itself and disappeared into the bushes. The bullet slammed into the tree trunk behind where the buck stood.

Elliot cursed and sighted his rifle. The bushes behind him were still rustling but he doubted anything would actually come out of them. The entire clearing smelled of gunshots now and the sound of his rifle probably scared all the deer nearby away. But then something burst out of the bushes beside him, and then something else did too. There was a streak of yellow and another streak of brown that raced across the clearing, disappearing into the trees on the other side. Elliot let off a round towards where the creatures, whatever they were, disappeared. He didn't hit anything apart from the tree trunk again.

Then the bushes rustled once more, exactly where the brown and yellow blurs disappeared. Elliot raised his rifle to his shoulder and stared through the sight at the bushes. Something brown slowly crept out, four legs and fur. There was a tail. It was big, bigger than a deer. He wondered whether he found a bear. He started to squeeze the trigger as it came to a stop. He searched for the best spot to make his mark, trying to remember everything that he could about shooting bears. Then another something came out of the bushes. This one was smaller and its fur was a bright, vibrant yellow. Elliot looked closer and almost dropped his gun.

"Well I'll be," he said quietly, "What in the heck are two dogs doing out here?"

He quickly lowered his rifle, all too aware that he was aiming it at someone's pets. He was looking at two dogs, one built like a bear and the other unmistakably a yellow Labrador.

"Bear!" a voice shouted, "Buddy, stay right there you little monsters,"

An old man burst out of the bushes from one side of the clearing and walked towards the dogs. They seemed to know him, they started prancing around him and leaping up at him. Their tails were wagging and they barked softly. Elliot stayed hidden, not wanting to intrude.

"You can't just go running off through the woods like this," the old man said gruffly, "It's hunting season, you'll get shot or worse, killed."

Elliot's stomach tightened at that. That was exactly what he almost did and he knew that the old man would have been so upset if he found his dogs dead. He was fussing around the dogs, wrapping something bright orange around their bodies. Elliot strained his ears to make out what he was saying to them.

"Well you two wear these now," the old man said, straightening up with a groan. He wagged a finger at the yellow dog, "And don't you go escaping this. You need it to be seen, I don't want you getting mistaken for some fancy deer and getting shot at. Bear, that goes for you too. If you're not careful someone will think you're a real bear and shoot you right between the eyes."

Elliot chuckled to himself. The brown dog did look pretty much like a bear. The old man started to walk away and the two dogs sat there, in the clearing looking at him and panting. He turned back to them.

"Well come on," he said, "You two are coming at least part way back with me. Come on, get."

He waved a hand at the path he took. The yellow dog barked and raced across to disappear between the trees and bushes. The brown dog followed at a more sedate pace, walking beside the man who was clearly his master.

Silence returned as the three left the clearing and Elliot let out a deep sigh. He took off his cap and mopped his brow. Then he remembered the message that he heard on the radio earlier. He reached for his own and pressed the button.

"This is Elliot," he said, "The dogs from earlier have been found and outfitted with vests. They're in bright orange. I repeat they are in bright orange."

He paused for a moment. Then he smiled and raised the radio to his mouth again.

"And the brown one does look like a bear so be careful. I almost shot them both."

The radio squawked a few times as other hunters responded. Elliot turned it to silent again and settled back into his hiding place. For the time being at least those dogs were safe and the hunters could focus on their real game at last. He hoped that the dogs would stay safe for the rest of the season and couldn't help but wonder if he would see them again.

Chapter 11

The Brown Family

One day, after several years had passed on The Hill, Bailey was exploring again. His life was happy and all his friends seemed happier when he was around. It was quite a while since he explored and tried to make new friends. He was happy with his current friends and created a routine where he went to visit them all and spend time with them. But he was starting to feel a little restless and wanted to see some new faces. So he took off into the woods once more and went to see who he could meet.

This time he went in a new direction. He caught a few smells through the years with his sharp nose but recently they become stronger and he could smell other dogs. It was a long time since he made friends with new dogs and he wanted to see if they were friendly like Bear or mean like Shadow. It was a sunny day, bright and warm. As he got closer to wherever the smells came from they got stronger and Bailey started to hear the sounds of laughter and dogs barking.

***

Travis and Tammy Brown lived in a little trailer on the edge of The Hill. It was a small home and they didn't have much money so the furniture inside was worn down and old. But there was a lot of love and that more than made up for everything else.

Travis wasn't as active as he once was which made him very sad. He was a hard worker and a happy, loving father. He would always come home from work, tired and aching, but no matter how tired he was and how much pain he was in he would still find time to play with the children, Kenny and Samantha. He would toss them in the air, wrestle with them, play the games that children liked to play. They were games that were full of energy and Travis always took the kids outside to play with them. This gave Tammy the room and space she needed to prepare the family's dinner and unwind after a day of her own work. The Browns were happy and loving despite their difficulties.

But things changed when Travis hurt his back. It was a terrible injury and he could no longer work. Standing for too long, even sitting for too long, left him in pain so bad that tears would come to his eyes. They tried everything that they could afford, from conventional medicine to acupuncture and aromatherapy. Nothing helped and Travis was forced to spend most of his day lying down in bed or on the sofa, worn and tired through it was. He couldn't play with his children any more, trying to toss them around like he once did left him unable to move for days afterwards. He couldn't work and he was forced to rely on support from the government, support which barely covered his medical bills, let alone their living costs.

So Tammy was forced to work longer hours, taking on more work than most other people could. She would come home exhausted and yet still find the time to make them all food and play with the children. Travis was saddened by this, he loved his family he couldn't help but feel guilty that he was simply a burden on them all now. He couldn't support them like he was supposed to, he couldn't even help his wife with the children. But he did what he could and showed his love for them in other ways. Travis would help Kenny with his homework, the little boy sitting on the floor by the sofa so that his dad could see what he was struggling with. He would settle Sam on the sofa by his side and read to her from her favorite story book, making sure that she could see the pictures. Money was tight, the costs of raising two young children rising ever higher and higher.

Things were made even harder by the fact that Sam was autistic. It meant that she needed to go to a special school, a place where the teachers were trained to handle children with special needs and understood how to help them learn. The Browns tried sending Sam to a regular school, the same one that Kenny went to, but after she came home every day for a week in tears and covered in mud where the other children pushed her down they decided it was worth it to send her to a school where she could be loved and protected.

But the special school cost money, money that they couldn't really spare. The Browns knew it was for the best and even Kenny tried to help when he overheard his parents talking about the cost. He brought out his piggy bank, with the few nickels it held and gave it to his parents in an attempt to help. They were touched by the gesture, Tammy was almost in tears and tried to refuse. But Kenny was determined to help his little sister, he loved her so much and Tammy and Travis realized that sending Sam to a school that was right for her was more important than making sure that their clothes were new and trendy and their appliances were all new.

The Browns did not have a television, only a radio that Kenny discovered on one of his forages through the yard sales in town. Although the trailer was old and drafty it was warm, cozy and filled with love. Kenny didn't need the television, even when he watched it at his friends' houses, it was boring and nowhere near as exciting as real life. He had two dogs to play with, the Brown's family dogs, Rosco and Chip, two mongrels that Travis found coming home from work before he hurt his back. Kenny entertained himself for hours exploring the woods with those dogs and teaching them tricks. He learned to track animals, using books that he borrowed from the library, he climbed trees and built forts. He was a boy of a different era and he didn't care.

Life for Sam wasn't so happy and carefree. She saw the world differently than other people. She didn't think in the same way that other people did. But thankfully she didn't know or understand or particularly care what it was that her family were missing out on. She loved her parents even if she didn't show it, and she loved Kenny and liked to watch him play. But she was scared of everything and never wandered far from the trailer, even when Kenny or Tammy was with her. The dogs scared her so much that she would run and hide if they ever got too close. And she never said a word.

***

Bailey crouched in the bushes near the trailer. These people were different from everyone else. There was no hum of electricity that seemed to hang around other people's homes, not the usual strong hum at any rate. This hum was low and subtle, almost unnoticeable. More importantly they were all outside. There was a man, lying flat on his back on an old lawn chair. Bailey thought that it looked like one of the ones that Mark threw away a few months ago and it certainly smelled faintly of him. There was a boy, running around and laughing as two small brown dogs chased him and jumped at the sticks that he was holding in each hand. Bailey almost wanted to join them. There was a woman on a blanket watching her son and smiling fondly. And there was a little girl, sitting on the woman's knee. She wasn't watching the boy, she buried her face in her mother's chest and her hands were holding on tightly to her mother's cardigan. Bailey could smell the fear on her from where he was hiding and realized that she didn't like dogs.

He stayed where he was and continued to watch this small and happy family. The trailer had the scent of oldness about it and their clothes did too. He was reminded of Old Man Joe and the simple way that he lived and figured that they had a similar attitude toward him. But they seemed happier somehow, more complete and friendly than Joe ever was.

As Bailey watched, the boy fell to the ground and lay there, panting for breath even as he kept laughing. The two dogs pounced on him and licked at him, their tails wagging harder than ever. The boy laughed and gently pushed them away. They raced off to lay in the shade of the trailer and Bailey noticed that the little girl let go of her mother once the dogs were gone. She moved from her mother's lap and sat on the blanket. The boy climbed to his feet, no longer out of breath and walked over to a patch of flowers that were growing on the edge of the grassy clearing. He pulled some of them up and walked back to the blanket.

"Look Sam," he said gently, lovingly, "Look at all the pretty colors. Aren't they nice?"

Bailey watched as the girl reached out and gently touched the flowers. She looked at them closely, ran her fingers over the petals. He realized that there was something different about her, something odd that he never saw in a human before. He didn't care, for some reason he actually liked it. He not only found new people he liked but he found a new kind of person. He wanted to see what the little girl was like.

The girl smiled and carefully took a flower from her brother's hand and held it close to her chest. She stroked the petals like she were stroking a pet and smiled at the boy again. The boy smiled back, widely, more widely than ever. He looked at his mother and she too was smiling. The two adults caught each other's eyes and their smiles tightened a little. Bailey sat up, his head cocked to one side. They were happy but they were sad at the same time and they were trying to hide it.

Bailey decided these people would be his new friends.

***

It was Rosco and Chip who first noticed the yellow dog coming out from between the bushes. They sat up and stared at him but made no move to run to him. They learned a long time ago that too many sudden movements would upset Sam and now moved carefully and slowly if she couldn't see them.

"Look Mom!" Kenny shouted, pointing at the dog, "It's a dog!"

"So I see," Tammy said. She gently took the flower that Sam was offering her. "I wonder where he came from,"

"Do you think he's friendly?" Kenny asked.

He already climbed to his feet and walked towards the new dog.

"Careful Kenny," Travis said warningly, "You don't know whose dog that is or if it's safe."

"He seems friendly," Kenny said, ignoring his dad's words.

He held out his hand and walked closer to the yellow dog. Behind him Sam climbed into her mother's lap again, holding on to her clothes. She hated dogs, they were scary and this yellow dog was the biggest one she ever saw. The yellow dog walked towards Kenny slowly, copying how the other two dogs moved when they weren't playing with Kenny. The boy's hand settled on his head and scratched his ears. The yellow dog whined softly and his tail wagged hard. He leaned into the petting and his mouth hung open.

"He is friendly!" Kenny cried.

He turned to look at his parents with happiness.

"Can we keep him?" he asked excitedly, "I bet he doesn't eat much,"

"A dog that size will eat more than Rosco and Chip put together," Travis said sternly. Then his face brightened a little, "And I think he already has a home buddy. Look how well looked after he looks,"

"Oh…" Kenny said sadly.

His dad was right of course, the dog was well fed if a little overweight and his coat gleamed brightly in the sunshine. A dog without a home wouldn't look like that he realized.

"But why is he here then if he has a home?" Kenny asked, "Do you think he ran away?"

"I doubt it," Travis said kindly, "I think he just likes to explore. Tell you what, you can play with him but you have to let him go when he wants to go home. Ok?"

"Ok dad," Kenny said. He turned to the dog with a wide smile, "Can you do any tricks?!"

***

Bailey kept going back to the Brown's trailer after that. It was the longest walk of all that he took to see his friends but it was well worth it in his opinion. They didn't give him a name but whenever he came around they were happy to see him, even Rosco and Chip. Sam still hid from him at first but as he visited more and more often she would stop running away and stay where she was.

Bailey liked the Browns. They were a kind and loving family and they made him feel like one of them. He realized that Travis couldn't really move and if it was a rainy day he would sit by the man and let him play with his ears. Sometimes he would explore the woods with Kenny, stopping the young boy from getting too close to anything dangerous. And he would fetch things for Tammy when she was doing chores around the house, gently picking up clothes in his mouth to take them to the washing machine for her.

They loved him and Bailey loved them back.

***

The more that the yellow dog visited, the more that Sam got used to him. She didn't normally like dogs, they mostly scared her, but the more that she saw of this dog the more that she liked him. She liked his yellow fur that looked really soft and was the color of the sun. It even shone like the sun when the dog was outside. She liked that the yellow dog never came too close to her, making sure that there was always a big space between them. It was like he was doing his best not to scare her. She liked his big brown eyes that seemed to see more than other dogs. They were shiny eyes with the same color as chocolate.

After a while, when the yellow dog didn't come to visit for a few days Sam started to feel very sad. It wasn't the usual sad that made her want to scream and shout and throw herself around. This was the sadness she felt when she went to school and said good bye to Mommy, Daddy and Kenny. She missed the yellow dog, seeing him and watching him pretending to be a person. And then he came back and all those feelings disappeared.

Now she was happy, she felt safe, a feeling that she didn't even realized was missing, and she felt almost normal. The day that the yellow dog came back she decided that it was time to see if his fur was as soft as it looked. She carefully walked towards him, still a little scared. She knew that her family was all watching her, they always did when she did something that she didn't normally do. She stretched out her hand, her fingertips inches from the fur that looked as soft as her favorite teddy bear. The dog was sitting still, very still, stiller than she had ever seen a dog sit. He was watching her, like he was waiting to see what she would do.

She kept walking forward and finally her finger tips sank into the yellow dog's fur. It was even softer than she imagined. She ran her fingers through it, feeling the strands rubbing against her skin. She was surprised that she liked the feeling so much, the softness that tickled her palms. On the rather occasions that she touched Rosco or Chip, purely by accident, their fur felt rough and wiry. But the yellow dog had soft fur, long and flowing that made pretty patterns when she moved her fingers through it.

Sam used both hands to pet the dog, enjoying the feeling more and more the longer than she did it. Her parents were watching and Tammy clutched at Travis when Sam smiled and pressed herself against the dog. Travis raised up a hand and gripped his wife's fingers, squeezing them gently. Kenny was watching his sister with wide eyes and when she moved her arms to wrap them around the yellow dog's neck and hug him the little boy's smile appeared, big and wide and joyful.

***

Bailey made sure that he stayed still when the little girl came towards him. He enjoyed the petting and stroking that she was doing but he didn't want to scare her away. So he kept his tail as still as he could. She looked scared when she first came up to him, almost like she couldn't believe what she was doing. But still she kept coming and Bailey watched her, ready to run if she decided she still didn't like dogs and started to cry. He was surprised when she kept stroking him and he almost yelped with shock when she wrapped her arms around his neck and hugged him.

Then as quickly as it began, it was over. Sam ran away, giggling so quietly that only Bailey, Rosco and Chip could hear her. Her parents watched her go in amazement. Bailey stood and took a few steps after her but heard her bedroom door shut loudly so he stopped. He looked at Travis, worried that he did something wrong but Travis was just staring at him with wide tear filled eyes and a big smile on his face.

"Looks like you're more than just a dog, boy," Travis said. He laughed and ruffled the fur on Bailey's head with a wide palm, "You're a good dog, a very good dog."

Bailey relaxed into the cuddles he was getting, a little startled when Kenny threw his arms around his neck and then even more surprised when Tammy did the same thing. Then he was released and Kenny was calling him to come outside and play. He happily followed, tail wagging hard. He did something amazing and was happy, even if he didn't know quite what it was that he did.

***

When he came to see the Browns the next day they were out in the garden, just as they were when he first visited. Rosco and Chip were playing with Kenny and Sam sat beside her mother. Bailey was a little surprised that she wasn't on her mother's lap like she usually was but then he realized that she was no longer as afraid of dogs as she once was. He trotted slowly out of the bushes and came to lie beside Sam. He moved slowly and carefully, making sure that she could see him the entire time. He knew from experience that going behind her or appearing suddenly scared her more than anything and once or twice she even ran away to hide inside the trailer.

When he sat beside Sam she smiled at him and reached out a small hand to pat him on the head. It was almost shy, the way that she petted him, like a toddler discovering an animal's fur for the first time. She pulled away quickly when Bailey leaned into her hand, holding her hand tightly to her chest but smiling at him. She looked happy, pleased with herself even and Bailey decided to lay on his side next to her, his back to her so she could pet him if she wanted to.

They lay there in the sun quietly, listening to Rosco and Chip barking, Kenny laughing and Travis and Tammy talking quietly among themselves. Bailey felt Sam's little hand on his head again, gently patting him and stroking along his fur. His tail wagged lazily. He was happy and comfortable, surrounded with people who loved him.

Eventually lying on his side got painful and he rolled on to his stomach. He raised his head up and sniffed the air. It was going to rain soon, he could smell it. But nothing else seemed to care about this and butterflies were still fluttering around from flower to flower. He realized that Sam was watching them intently. She was smiling at the colors of their wings and Travis and Tammy were smiling at each other and at Sam as she enjoyed the outdoors.

One flew closer and closer, fluttering through the air blown by an invisible breeze. It landed gently on Bailey's nose, its little legs tickling the bare skin. He kept still and looked at it.

Then he heard a giggling sound, giggling that he had never heard before. It was Sam. Travis and Tammy were staring at her in surprise. Kenny stopped his game with the other dogs and watched his sister.

"Doggy!" Sam cried suddenly.

The butterfly took off unexpectedly and Bailey sneezed.

"Doggy," Sam cried again.

She threw herself at Bailey and wrapped her arms around his neck, burying her face in his fur. Bailey looked over her shoulder and saw Tammy and Travis crying. Tammy was gripping Travis' hand tightly, the knuckles white. Her other hand was over her mouth. Tears of sheer joy streamed down both of their faces and they were smiling so widely that Bailey was surprised that their faces didn't hurt.

"Doggy, doggy, doggy," Sam repeated over and over.

She was still hugging Bailey's neck and was rubbing her face all over his fur. Kenny ran over, smiling but Rosco and Chip hung back, knowing that they shouldn't scare the little girl. Kenny was smiling and knelt beside his sister. He stroked Bailey's head gently.

"Way to go champ," he said, "You got her talking at last."

The family huddled together around Bailey and Sam, tears of joy and laughter falling down their faces. Bailey lay there and soaked it all in.

***

Bailey was sad to leave that day. The Browns seemed so happy and Sam barely let him out of her sight. She was obsessed with him now it seemed. She just kept stroking him and petting him. She even went so far as to lean against him when he lay on the ground. He liked her light weight on him, the way that she seemed to relax completely when he was around. It was new and strange and exciting and it seemed to make Travis and Tammy happy. Bailey liked making his people happy.

***

The next day he returned, wondering whether it had just been a one off event. As soon as he set paw in the clearing he realized it hadn't been. Sam came racing out of the trailer, arms outstretched towards him. He slowly plodded forwards and she threw her arms around his neck, just as she did the day before.

"Champ!" she cried.

Bailey barked softly and Sam giggled.

From that point on Bailey's name at the Brown's house was Champ. He was Sam's dog. She would only pet him, not Rosco or Chip. She would only smile at him and Bailey realized that she only talked when he or a reminder of him was around. And she talked a lot. So Bailey decided to make sure that the trailer was full of things that made Sam think of him and talk.

He kept coming to visit Sam and each time he would bring something that he found when he was exploring somewhere else. Once it was a toy that someone left at Ma's house and she threw it away. Bailey took it gently from the pile and disappeared into the woods. Ma didn't chase him for it so he figured that it was ok. Another time it was a flower from Charlie's garden, one of the prettiest ones that he could find. Lulu helped him decide, she sniffed at all the flowers and found one that was just right. Lulu had a better eye for pretty things than Bailey did, he decided. Charlie had noticed that Bailey wouldn't leave the flower alone so he carefully cut its stem and handed it to Bailey to take in his mouth. Once Bailey even stole one of Mark's old socks. Mark had tossed it to one side, grumbling about the hole and Bailey had picked it up and disappeared. Mark shouted after him but Bailey really wanted to give the sock to Sam.

All of the gifts were brought carefully to the Browns and Bailey, or Champ as he was called there, each placed gently down at Sam's feet. She would pick the gifts up, examine them carefully before eventually smiling. Bailey was allowed inside her room a few weeks later and saw all of the presents that he had bought her, neatly displayed. The pretty flower were pressed and now hung in a frame beside her bed, the sock had buttons sewn on to it and Sam made it make strange noises at it. The toy was polished and fixed and was on the small table that served as Sam's desk.

Bailey liked that she was keeping his presents when it would be so easy to throw them away. He loved Sam, and Tammy, and Travis, and Kenny, and even Rosco and Chip. He loved that he made them all so happy and he really loved that they were a big family with not much to spare and they were still willing to share their love with him. He liked going to the Brown's trailer and soaking in the love and laughter while Sam hung around his neck or rode him like a pony.

Every time he returned it would take him a little longer to get there than it once did because Bailey was checking each of his friends' houses for something to bring. He never came to see Sam without a present and she was always happy to see her Champ, with or without a gift. Bailey just liked that the presents made her smile bigger.

Chapter 12

The City Folk

Bailey knew that there was a small house on the Hill that people only lived in from time to time. He passed it on his travels, quite a few times and although it smelled faintly of people the smell was never very strong and the house was completely quiet. He could smell dogs. There were scratches in the mud of the garden that told him there were at least three dogs that ran around. The different scents told him that too. Bailey caught the smell of the city once or twice, the same smell that used to surround him back when he lived with Amanda. He didn't like that smell too much, not then and not now. It was too strong, too sour and acidic in his nose. It made his nostrils sting and twitch and made him sneeze. It was fainter than it was when he lived with Amanda, diluted by all of the country smells but it still made him sneeze a little.

Bailey tried to see who was in the house, who the dogs were and whether they were nice or mean. He hoped that they were nice. But whenever he did try to visit the house and meet the people they were either not there for a very long time or they just left. That made him a little sad but he knew that sooner or later he would meet them. So he kept going back, in the early mornings, hoping to see one of those big metal cars outside that would tell him that someone was there.

***

Virginia and Wilson loved the country but they lived and worked in the city. They lived all the way in Washington DC but they decided that they wanted a nice house to live in once they retired and could have a slower way of life. The city was busy, full of life and people going from place to place all of the time. No one really knew each other and everyone was always on the go. There was no time. In the country, things were different and that was what Virginia and Wilson loved about it. They wanted to avoid the people in the country however, having grown tired of being surrounded by people back in Washington DC. So when they saw the house on The Hill for sale, miles of land between all of the other houses, they snapped it up without a moment's hesitation.

They weren't ready to retire yet, their lives were still too busy and Wilson's career was finally going the way they always dreamed it would go. But they enjoyed the house, in their own way, visiting most weekends. They would bring their three German Shepherd dogs with them, putting them in the back of the car for the 5 hour trip to The Hill whenever they could spare the time. The countryside was quiet and gave the dogs a chance to run around without

Virginia having to worry about them getting hit by a car or something else terrible happening.

Their lives were busy with more than work. They didn't have children, their dogs were essentially their children, but they had a life of travel and excitement. They would see shows in the theater, sitting in their fancy clothes and watching highly trained actors sing and dance and feel the emotion that they were portraying. They would take cruises, visiting far off exotic lands while traveling in the lap of luxury. They would travel, taking long holidays in sunny places, just relaxing and unwinding in a slower way of life than that of the city. They enjoyed it all, loved it all really but it was only in the country where they felt completely at home.

Virginia and Wilson had a wonderful marriage. They met each other at the perfect time, the best points in their respective lives. They fell in love instantly and although they had a few rocky patches, as any marriage does, it was a whirlwind romance that lasted and lasted. They were still very much in love and the house on The Hill was a way for them to prepare for the rest of their lives together.

The house was small and neat, nestled within the woods and surrounded by a patch of green grass. The roads were little more than dirt tracks and the closest neighbor was over a mile away. Virginia and Wilson loved it from the first moment they saw it. The times that they spent at the house were the happiest of their lives together, even more relaxing than the many cruises and spa holidays that they had taken together. They were completely alone you see, they didn't have to interact with people, they rarely even saw anyone else. And that was the way that they liked it, it was why they bought the house.

***

Virginia sat out on the porch early one morning. They arrived at the house late the night before and Wilson was still sleeping. The long drive had exhausted him but Virginia had been luckier, having the chance to doze a time or two on the trip. So now she was watching her dogs run around, enjoying the space and freedom and fresh air. She sipped at her coffee and smiled as the dogs frolicked together and barked happily.

It was a wonderful morning. The sun was just clearing the trees and shining down on the grass which still sparkled with morning dew. There were a few birds flying around catching insects and more were singing among the trees. The day held the promise of being warm and fresh and Virginia loved it. There was none of the closeness that came in the city, just fresh air, wide open spaces and countryside for miles and miles around. She sighed with contentment and leaned back in her chair.

She sat up, watching the dogs carefully when they stopped running around and stood in the middle of the garden, staring at the woods. She heard the door behind her open and smiled tightly when Wilson kissed her gently on the head.

"What's going on?" he asked as he sat down and poured his own cup of coffee, "What's up with the dogs?"

"I don't know..." Virginia said, "They just started staring into the woods."

"Maybe they saw a rabbit," Wilson said with a carefree shrug, "The woods are full of them."

"I don't think so," Virginia said, "They would have been barking by now."

The couple watched their dogs for a few minutes more and then something moved in among the trees. They stared, mouths falling open, as a yellow Labrador came out of the trees. He was wet and covered in mud. His tail was wagging happily and his mouth was hanging open like he was smiling. Virginia and Wilson climbed to their feet and slowly made their way down the porch steps towards their own dogs. The entire time the yellow dog just sat and watched them, mouth still hanging open in his happy smile. Virginia raised a hand to her nose as she got closer and gave a cry of disgust.

"Yuck!" she cried, "He smells disgusting. What is that odor?"

"Smells like fox poop," Wilson said, his own nose wrinkled up.

The yellow dog barked and before Virginia or Wilson could stop them their dogs raced over to him and welcomed him. They leapt around him, rubbing themselves against him and sniffing and licking at his fur.

"Well I'll be," Wilson said in amazement.

The dogs never seemed to like other dogs, it usually took them several weeks before they were so welcoming to newcomers. But now the dogs were leaping around the dog like they had known him forever, as though he were an old friend that they hadn't seen in a long time. And the yellow dog seemed just as happy to see them too.

"I'll get the hose," Wilson said with a sigh. "The dogs are covered in that stuff now and I don't want them tracking it into the house."

"Wait!" Virginia cried, grabbing his arm, "Shouldn't we call the dog catcher or something? He's a loose dog, who knows where he's from,"

"Leave it be," Wilson said eventually, "He's probably got a home. He looks well fed enough. Besides things are different here in the country. We don't want to be going and upsetting the locals."

"Hmmm," Virginia said.

She watched the dogs playing together and eventually let go of her husband's arm. He headed off to the side of the house, to get the hose and she worried. She still had the mentality of the city, it was deeply ingrained in her. It felt wrong to have a dog running loose, it just wasn't done in Washington. You never knew where the dog came from, what diseases it might have, whether it could turn savage at any moment.

Wilson returned with the hose before she could act on her fears. The water rained down over the yellow dog, and Misty and King and Chewy. They loved it, they started to run around in the water that fell from the sky, trying to bite at the streams. Slowly the mud and other substances washed away from the yellow dog's fur, leaving behind only yellow. The water ran dark and dingy across the grass and into the trees. Still the dogs raced around together, in and out of the water, their tails wagging. They shook of the water on their coats, sprinkling Virginia and Wilson with a light shower. The two laughed at the dogs' antics and Virginia's worries faded a little.

"I'm going to go and get them some treats," She said eventually.

She disappeared into the house and moments later returned with a milk bone for each. The dogs lined up, taking the treat gently from her hand. When she got to Yellow Dog, as she was now calling him in her mind, she was surprised. The dog sat down and gently rested one paw on her hand, asking for his treat. She laughed and held the milk bone out. Yellow Dog took it from her hand and lay on the grass as he crunched it down.

"Look at that!" she cried to Wilson, "Yellow Dog does tricks!"

"I wonder who taught him that one," Wilson said with a smile.

"Probably his owner," she suggested.

"So Yellow Dog is his name now?" Wilson asked "It fits,"

"Yes it does," Virginia said with a smile.

***

Bailey liked his name of Yellow Dog at the city folk's house. He liked Virginia and Wilson too. They gave him tasty treats and cuddles whenever he appeared. Misty, Chewy and King were great fun too. He wanted to take them on adventures but whenever he tried to lead them away from the garden and into the woods Virginia would cry out. The dogs were good dogs, like Bailey knew they would be, and they always stopped when she called their names. Bailey figured that it was just because Virginia didn't know that the woods were really safe that she didn't let them go exploring. He hoped that she would eventually find that out and she would let the three German Shepherds explore with Bailey. Maybe one day they could all run through the woods like Bailey used to do with Bear before he got too old to explore any more.

***

Virginia loved having Yellow Dog visit. He brightened their lives and was always so friendly. He would do funny expressions with his face and always seemed to have a doggy smile. There was another reason that she loved Yellow Dog coming to visit. He helped her rediscover her love of photography.

She really enjoyed taking pictures when she was young. Her camera was never too far from her side. She had many albums full of the photos that she took over her years. But as time passed life got in the way and Virginia found herself taking less and less photos. Eventually it got to the point where she only brought her camera out for their holidays or on special occasions. Photography started to feel like a chore and she lost the love that once burned so strongly.

But with Yellow Dog around that love was reignited. There were so many funny and entertaining things that Yellow Dog did, and got Misty, King and Chewy to do, that she wanted to memorialize them in pictures. So the camera came out again and she started to take more and more photos. Soon Virginia started to keep a camera at the house on The Hill, even when she was back in DC, the camera at hand ready for her to grab, point and shoot.

"These are so wonderful," Wilson said one afternoon as they looked through the prints, "I can't believe you managed to catch them like this."

The photo in question was of Misty, Chewy and King all curled up on the garden. They were covering Yellow Dog up, the pups having collapsed into a dog pile after playing a very exciting game of chase. Virginia captured the whole game with her camera but this photograph was by far her favorite.

"Wait!" Wilson said suddenly as he looked through another one, "You let them go into the woods?!"

"They didn't go far," Virginia said with a shrug, "They stayed where I could see them. But Yellow Dog really wanted to take them in there so I let him. He kept them close and they all came back when I called,"

"But it might not be safe in there!" Wilson cried out again, "Who knows what or who might be in those woods,"

"Wilson, dear," Virginia said fondly, "Yellow Dog comes through those woods every day and he's always fine. I think he likes to run around them all the time. That's why he's always so muddy. He knows the woods and I don't think he'd let anything happen to his friends."

Wilson hummed in disagreement but didn't say anything else. It was clear to him that Virginia was growing more relaxed about country life and that was something that he couldn't argue with. The change between country and city living was vast and hard to accept and even harder to get used to. It was no lie between them that Virginia was having a little trouble adjusting. If Yellow Dog was helping her get used to living in the country then Wilson wasn't going to stop them.

***

As Yellow Dog's visits increased Virginia learned to relax even more. She was hesitant at first to let the dogs disappear into the woods with Yellow Dog but slowly she got used to the idea. She let them go further and further into the woods until eventually they would be gone for hours with Yellow Dog. At first she worried, about the dogs and about Yellow Dog, but he always brought them back to her, safe and sound and in one piece.

Even when Yellow Dog wasn't around Virginia started to relax more. She would leave the door to the house open and after making sure that their gate was closed she would let Misty, Chewy and King come and go from the house to the garden as they pleased. It was a new experience for her, letting her dogs have so much freedom. In the city she never dared allow it. She worried about the safety of her dogs, whether they might get on to the road and get hit by a car or get attacked by another dog. At one point, after a string of dog abductions she worried that the dogs would be grabbed and dragged into a van to be sold off and never seen again.

She also worried about her own safety. She didn't feel right in the city, leaving the door to her house open. The garden to her city house had been secure the idea of leaving the back door open terrified her. All it would take would be one opportunistic person to spot the open door and she could have ended up with who knows what kind of strangers invading her home.

But Yellow Dog helped her get used to the idea of doing that at The Hill. He was always coming and going, disappearing off to wherever it was that he lived. Sometimes when she was driving into town to pick up groceries she would catch sight of his yellow fur in the woods on one side of the road or the other, racing through the trees. Sometimes on her drives she would spot him walking along the road with another dog by his side, one that she didn't recognize. She would see him with different people all of the time, some old and slow, others young children that raced along with him at their side.

They all seemed friendly and welcoming, happy and carefree. Virginia wondered whether that was the work of Yellow Dog or if it was just the way that the world worked around The Hill.

Yellow Dog almost always appeared when she was taking the dogs for walks along the surrounding roads. He knew exactly when to come, just before they were about to leave. Once or twice she tried to put a lead around his neck but he would dance around, avoiding her hands and enjoying their new game. She would quickly grow tired of this and decide to take the dogs for a walk even if Yellow Dog wasn't on a lead.

She kept King and Chewy and Misty on leads, the habit so ingrained into her. She was worried that they would see something in the woods and give chase, disappearing among the trees. Yellow Dog never seemed to do that, he walked with them all with no lead on. He would simply trot along just ahead of them, sniffing at the verge, marking his territory and sometimes bouncing ahead. He would always stop before he got too far and wait, looking back at them over his shoulder with a doggy smile.

Slowly Virginia started letting the dogs off the lead for longer and longer periods of time and was more and more surprised. Whenever it looked like King was getting ready to chase after a rabbit or something among the trees Yellow

Dog would bark and get between King and the Rabbit. If Misty got too distracted by a scent and began to fall behind everyone else, Yellow Dog would race up to her and gently push her to get moving again. Chewy always stayed close to Virginia, walking at her heel but Yellow Dog slowly started to coax him to run a little ahead of her. She would smile and laugh every time Chewy stopped to look back and wait for her and Yellow Dog would bump him gently and get him moving again.

It soon got to the point where she didn't even bother with leads whenever Yellow Dog joined them on their walks. She trusted that Misty King and Chewy would stay nearby and not run too far away. And she trusted that Yellow Dog would help her to look after her precious pets. And eventually she started to leave the leads behind even when Yellow Dog wasn't with them on their walks. Misty would fall behind now and then but Chewy would quickly trot back to get her moving again. King might want to chase after a rabbit from time to time but Misty would bark at him and he would return to the pack. Chewy would run further and further ahead, no longer stuck to Virginia, as long as the others ran with him. They looked after each other. Yellow Dog taught them to and Virginia loved him for that.

Yellow Dog was teaching Wilson and Virginia all about the real country way of life, the relaxed attitude and the slow pace that everyone seemed to follow. The couple grew more and more used to living their lives slow when they were on The Hill, they took their time getting to places and moved without hurry or any real purpose. The Hill quickly became their refuge from city life and it was the only place on earth where they felt like they could really relax and be themselves.

***

One day Virginia and Wilson were driving back from the town with some groceries in the trunk of their car. It was a cool day but sunny and they decided to leave the dogs at home, leaving the door open and letting them do as they wanted. Months ago, before meeting Yellow Dog, the couple would never have dreamed about doing such a thing but now it was like second nature to them, something they actively stopped themselves from doing when they were back in DC.

That day Wilson was driving and they were taking their time. The countryside around the road was beautiful, with meadows of flowers and grass on one side and tall towering trees on the other.

"Oh look at that!" Virginia cried, pointing ahead of them,

"What's that sign say?" Wilson asked, leaning forward and squinting at the handmade sign, "Honey, $2 a jar? Want some honey, honey?"

Virginia smiled and nodded so Wilson turned their car up the small driveway that led away from the dirt road they were on. The drive was a little pot holed but otherwise ok and the car rolled slowly down it, bouncing the couple around. A small hut appeared, rustic and unique. A man sat on the porch with a shotgun on his knee. Wilson stopped and climbed out slowly. He motioned at Virginia to stay in the car.

"Sir?" he called gently.

"Yeah?" the old man said, "What do you want?"

"We saw the sign at the end of your drive?" Wilson said, "We wanted to buy some honey,"

"Ah," the old man said, "I forgot that sign was there. Hold on a minute."

The old man slowly climbed to his feet, still gripping the shotgun. Wilson's eyes were locked on it and the old man caught the direction he was looking in.

"Oh don't mind this," the man said, propping the shot gun against the hut, "I keep it to scare the bears away. Sometimes they get too close and try to get into my hives. Can't have them eating my honey now, can I?"

Wilson sighed with relief and motioned for Virginia to climb out of the car.

"I'm Wilson," he said, stepping forward to shake the man's hand, "And this is my wife Virginia,"

"Joe," the old man said simply, "You must be them city folk I've heard a bit of talk about. Bought the old Ridgeley place three miles off right? Only come here now and then,"

"News travels... slow around here," Virginia said,

"I don't get out much and you've not exactly made yourselves known to the locals," Joe said with a shrug, "How's The Hill treating you?"

"It's nice," Wilson said, "Right now the house is just a holiday home. Soon it's going to be where we retire to. We like it here, nice and calm and relaxed."

"Aye, that it is," Joe said. "Well, I better get you that honey. How many jars did you want?"

"Three please," Virginia said, "I like to use it when I try to bake,"

"Best honey in three counties," Joe said, "Well worth using in your baking Ma'am,"

Joe disappeared into the house and they could hear a little clattering now and then. Once or twice the old man swore loudly and then shouted his apologies quickly. Virginia and Wilson giggled with each other and looked around Joe's property.

"Hey, isn't that Yellow Dog?" Wilson asked, pointing at a speck that was moving among the trees. "What's he doing all the way out here?"

"Maybe he's Joe's dog," Virginia said with a shrug, "He's got to live somewhere around here, isn't that what you said?"

"Maybe," Wilson agreed. "I don't know."

The couple was interrupted before they could discuss it more by the return of Joe. He was holding three jars of honey, just as Virginia asked. In his other hand was a small brown paper bag.

"Here's a little something else," he said, holding it out to Wilson, "A bit of jerky for you to chew on when you're driving back to the big city. I smoke it myself with a secret recipe I got from my granddaddy."

"Well thank you!" Wilson said, happily taking both things, "How much do I owe you?"

As Wilson and Joe talked prices and exchanged pleasantries Virginia continued to watch Yellow Dog in the woods. He was slowly getting closer and there was another dog at his side, a great big brown beast of a dog. It was moving slow. It was tired and old. She smiled as Yellow Dog clearly didn't run too fast and stayed by the side of his friend. Clearly Joe looked after Yellow Dog well and was a good master. She was happy that there was someone else out there looking after Yellow Dog just as he looked after other people.

***

Bailey raised his head as he heard the sound of an engine. He recognized that sound, it was the sound of Virginia and Wilson's car. They were driving away from Joe's house and he wondered what they wanted. Then Bear barked and Bailey raced back to walk beside his friend. They played too long in the woods and now Bear was tired and ready for a rest. Perhaps once he returned Bear to Joe Bailey would go and see Virginia and Wilson and play with Chewy, King and Misty. He hadn't seen them for a while.

As he got closer the scent of his friends grew stronger and lingered. He figured that they must have stayed there for a while and thrill of happiness raced through him. His friends were getting to know each other. Perhaps they would all be friends too. That was something Bailey would love.

Chapter 13

The Passing Years

Bailey was happy. He was quite possibly one of the happiest dogs on The Hill, if not the entire East Coast. It was quite possible that he was the happiest dog in the world. He had many names, many families and many friends. He visited them all as the years continued to pass by, seeing them, watching them, and playing with them. He made their lives happier and better and many were better people for having him in their lives.

As the years passed Mark matured and grew into a better person, mostly because of Bailey's help. The yellow dog taught him to laugh at himself and talk about his feelings. Bailey helped Mark more than any person ever did. Bailey had a secret life too, many secret lives that Mark knew nothing about. Most of Bailey's other families knew he was visiting people other than them. Bailey lived for these visits on the days when Mark and Ben traveled into the city to do their work. He was never lonely and always had someone to turn to if he wanted to spend time with people.

The woods were all around if he wanted to spend time by himself, exploring and sniffing out rabbits to chase.

Buddy kept going to see Old Man Joe, sharing a bacon breakfast and a roll in the nearby meadow with Bear. He was sad one day when he went to see Joe and found Bear no longer there. He let the old man hold him tight and cry into his fur as the man explained that Bear just got so old that he had lay down to sleep one night and never woke up. After that Buddy made sure to keep coming to see Old Man Joe, that he visited and brought some sunshine into his life. Joe missed Bear like crazy and although it was hard at first, seeing Buddy most days without Bear by his side it slowly got easier and easier. Joe started to realize that even with Bear gone he wasn't alone. It helped that the city folk would come and visit him from time to time and shared his grief. They even offered to find him a new dog but Joe was too sad and couldn't bear the thought of another dog taking Bear's place.

So he contented himself with Buddy's occasional company and having a dog around that wasn't actually his dog. Buddy felt like he owed it to Bear to keep Joe company too and he liked the old man. Whenever Joe started a new project, something that he was very fond of doing, Buddy would make sure that he was there, keeping an eye on Joe and making sure that the old man didn't get himself into any trouble that he couldn't get out of. And he liked the peace and quiet at Joe's house. He could just lie at Joe's feet and relax when he was tired or his bones were hurting. It was nice and companionably silent.

Sunshine kept paying a visit to see Lulu, swimming in their pond and enjoying the flowers in the garden. Charlie and Bob delighted in seeing Sunshine help Lulu get over her many fears and loved that she was no longer a trembling ball of fur. They could take her for longer walks now, even through the town and she no longer shook and whined with fear. And they knew that Sunshine was responsible for that. They gave him treats and cuddles, even put a fancy winter coat on him during a particularly cold winter. Of course Sunshine lost it within a few hours but they were happy that he let them put it on him at all.

Love always seemed to know when Marianne was sad and would appear, as if by magic. She started to keep a cookie or two in her cupboards and as soon as she saw him appear on the drive one would appear in her hand, ready for him to gently take. Love was happy to spend time with Marianne, especially when he knew that she was really missing her husband. He would stay the night, curled up beside her on her bed. He really enjoyed falling asleep with her fingers running through his fur and waking up with her arm wrapped around his neck. It made him feel loved and he would wake her with slobbery kisses.

She didn't reach for the wine bottle when she was feeling sad any more. Instead she would reach for her book and one of Love's cookies. She'd started eating them if Love didn't come and over time she developed the same taste for them as her husband. She socialized more, Love's visits encouraging her to take her dogs for walks and she met many of the other dog owners on The Hill. She and her friends sometimes spent evenings playing cards or chatting over tea and coffee instead of sitting at home alone with a bottle of wine. She knew Love was to thank for her new found freedom and lease on life.

Dingbat's timing was amazing. He always seemed to know when Amos was driving away for a long trip and he would appear right beside Axel. They would spend the nights lying side by side under the stars, just keeping each other company. Dingbat really liked doing that when it was hot because Amos' home was nice and cool, getting a breeze from the top of The Hill. Dingbat would tell Axel all about his walks, the people that he met and the friends that he made. Axel was still stuck by Amos' house, he never really got to go on walks anywhere other than along the road. So he lapped up Dingbat's stories and imagined all these people in his mind. He thought that he might have seen one or two of them wandering around from time to time actually.

Of course Dingbat didn't want to make Axel too sad with the stories of the wonderful things that he never saw for himself. So Dingbat made sure to include tales of the not so nice things that happened on his walks, like the raccoon that chased him through the woods for three miles. Or the bear that appeared right between him and his favorite drinking spot. He told Axel all about the men in the bright jackets with their shiny loud guns that appeared for a few weeks every year. Axel always wondered what those loud explosions were and wanted to go and investigate for himself. When Dingbat told him what the guns did and what happened to the animals that got in the way of the explosions Axel wasn't so keen any more. In fact he was quite glad that he didn't get to explore as much as Dingbat did.

There were a few more encounters with coyotes of course, the creatures getting too close to Amos house. They developed a system of working together to drive the rogue beasts away and made sure that they were never hurt like that first time. There were always signs of the coyote visits and Amos quickly discovered them when he came home. With each sign of these visits Amos grew a little nicer and kinder towards Axel. He would never be in the ranks of Ma and Pop or Virginia and Wilson when it came to owning a dog but he was getting better. And Dingbat made it happen. Axel owed the yellow dog his life several times over and they both knew it.

Happy kept visiting Cody as well, bringing joy to the young boy's life. Of course Cody grew older and his interests turned away from exploring and having adventures and towards new things like sports and girls. He still always made time for Happy and more often than not they would simply go for long walks through the woods together. Cody even introduced Happy to some of his friends from school and cemented his place in the school's hierarchy by showing off all of the tricks that Happy learned.

Happy was a little sad of course, when Cody no longer wanted to go fishing out on the lake or climb trees but he was content just to spend time with the boy. He liked to see how much Cody changed since they first met. He was no longer shy and sad, instead Cody became confident and friendly and full of smiles. There were still a few sad times of course, particularly around the time of the anniversary of his parents' deaths but Happy was there to cuddle and cry to. Happy was just glad to help and improve his friend's life.

Champ kept going to the Brown family as well. He continued to bring them presents, each one being taken by little Sam and put somewhere safe. She came out of her shell more and more for every year that passed. When once she only said a few words and those few words came whenever

Champ was around she was talking almost all the time now. They weren't always full sentences but they were enough to make herself understood and her parents seemed happier and more content than they were before.

Times were still hard of course but Champ and his effect on Sam brought a little bit of happiness to their lives that were missing before without them even realizing. That happiness made the hard times just that little bit easier to deal with. Even Travis wasn't as upset about being stuck on the couch all of the time when Champ was around. The dog liked to help out and would get things for the man so, even when he couldn't really move, he was still able to help around the house. Even if it was something as simple as peeling vegetables over his knees he could help and all because Champ was there to fetch anything that fell. Champ even taught Rosco and Chip to do the same things and they helped Travis and Tammy look after the children. Sam started to give them cuddles too, when Champ wasn't around. But Champ was always her number one favorite dog and she would drop everything when he turned up. Her parents didn't mind, after all he changed all of their lives.

Yellow Dog kept on visiting Virginia and Wilson too, along with their dogs, Chewy, King and Misty. Virginia relaxed about the dogs more and more, happy to leave the door open so that they could come and go whenever they pleased. She knew that Yellow Dog would always bring them back safe and sound. Yellow Dog helped the married couple get used to the slower pace of country life and helped them to relax. They enjoyed his visits so much that it made them never want to go back to the city. They would find reasons to stay at The Hill for longer and longer each time they visited but sadly they were always forced to return to the city. But it got harder every time and they would spend their time in the city dreaming of The Hill and the wonderful life that they were beginning to build there.

Spirit kept Officer Henderson on his toes too. He would lead him on wild chases through the woods and fields. He would trick Officer Henderson into chasing him for many miles, getting the man to exercise and work to catch Spirit. Officer Henderson enjoyed their games, dreading the day that he might finally catch Spirit. So he embraced the chase, tried to out think Spirit but the yellow dog was just too smart for him. Every time Officer Henderson thought that he cornered Spirit, he would somehow find a way to escape and disappear as fast as he appeared. It was fun and George actually found himself growing fond of Spirit. It didn't stop him doing his job. Spirit just helped him find some enjoyment that was missing before.

***

The years continued to pass and as all things do Bailey started to get older and older. He couldn't go as far as he once did. He couldn't run through the woods chasing rabbits or visit all of his friends in one day. His joints were sore and his eyes were starting to go. At first he tried to keep visiting all of his friends all of the time but he couldn't do it anymore. Slowly he started to only visit one or two of them in a day, three if it was a good day with little pain. But soon he found himself only able to visit one of his friends. He tried to cycle through them, visiting each one in turn. Then days would go by without Bailey leaving the house because his joints hurt so much.

It wasn't so bad. Ben and Mark's plumbing business was successful and they made a name for themselves as good, reliable plumbers. They were able to charge more money for fewer jobs. This meant that Mark didn't have to work as much in the city. He could spend more time at home, with Bailey. Bailey wasn't as boisterous as he once was, he now preferred to just sit by Mark and ask for cuddles. They enjoyed the peace and quiet together, with Mark reading, watching television or surfing the internet while Bailey sat by his side.

Of course there were still worries in Mark's life. Ben, like Bailey, was growing old and he caught an illness that just wouldn't shift. He had to go to the hospital to receive treatment and to run tests. The doctors couldn't seem to work out what was wrong with the man but they kept trying. So the hospital became Ben's second home and Mark stayed in the one that they built together and enjoyed Bailey's company.

If it happened earlier in their life together Mark would not really have had the chance to bond with Bailey. The dog would have been too busy exploring the area and making new friends. But now, with age making its slow creep up on him, Bailey was at home more and more. Mark remembered why they took in Bailey, it was the mischief and happiness that just seemed to pour out of the dog and affect anyone nearby. Mark started to explore The Hill too, taking Bailey on a few walks, worried that the dog wouldn't be able to come back. He met some of the people that he met before and got to know them all over again. He learned about them, caught up on things that he missed.

Everything that Mark loved about the Hill when he first moved there came rushing back to him. He didn't realize that the love faded away with the hum drum of the day to day and the repetition that his life took on. He would sit in his back garden in the mornings and remember as he watched Bailey wander around, smelling the flowers and enjoying himself.

The dog's slow waddle saddened him however. Bailey's walk was once excited, bouncy and easy. But now Bailey was slower and a little jerky. A few limps were developing in the way he walked. Mark knew what that meant but he didn't want to accept it, not really. He loved Bailey too much to accept that he was growing old. It was hard to see Bailey grow old as it was to see his Dad grow old. In a way, in Mark's mind, it was harder. Bailey was always so full of life, so excited and full of energy. Seeing him slow down and stop bouncing around just felt wrong. It wasn't right, the dog just walking and limping everywhere. He could only bark at the butterflies that landed on his nose or the rabbits that peeked at him from within the trees. He should be able to run and chase after them, to explore and race through the woods like he used to.

But there was nothing that Mark could do to stop it happening. Bailey would grow older and Mark could only make him comfortable.

***

Mark wasn't the only one on The Hill who realized that Bailey was getting older. Marianne noticed more and more gray hairs among Love's fur. Cody spotted that Happy struggled to get up the stairs to his bedroom. Joe realized that Buddy would just sit and watch rather than getting things for him like he used to. Travis wanted to cry when he heard the way that Champ groaned with pain when he tried to get the remote for him. Virginia and Wilson, Chewy, King and Misty realized that Yellow Dog wasn't bounding around like before, that his claws weren't clicking and clattering loudly on the wooden floors, they were just tapping steadily as he came to the door.

Ma and Pop knew too. They saw Bailey just sat by the fence, watching the foals running around and playing games among themselves. He would have once been right in among them, joining in. Now he sat watching, chin resting on one of the bars going between the posts. Now and then they heard him sigh. Even Shadow knew something was wrong. He stopped chasing Bailey, just gave him a cursory growl before walking away. Officer Henderson realized that he hadn't seen Spirit wandering around for months, at least not alone. Now whenever he saw Spirit there was a man at his side and the two would be slowly walking down the road.

Charlie and Bob noticed that Sunshine wasn't splashing around the pond like before. Lulu was always the one that raced ahead and leapt into the water now. Sunshine just followed behind slowly and slid into the water. Usually Sunshine would groan as he moved or lay down too, speaking of a pain that no one else knew. Axel barely saw Dingbat any more. His friend only came to visit when it was a very warm day and an equally warm night. The coyotes would come and they would chase them off together but Dingbat would always collapse and fall asleep after. There wasn't the speed that Dingbat used to have even if he was still just as fearsome. Amos saw Dingbat more too, the dog too slow to race away and disappear like he used to.

And eventually he visited them less and less. Days, weeks, would go by between Bailey's visits to his friends. They would miss him, they would know that he wasn't there, particularly the other dogs, but there was nothing that they could do to change it. All of Bailey's friends on The Hill knew that he was getting old. He wasn't visiting as much as before, that he was eating less and he moved slower than he ever. They realized that he was probably staying at home, wherever it was, because they weren't seeing him. They couldn't blame him. He had done so much for them that it was only fair that he could have a nice rest as he got older.

All the logic in the world didn't make the reality easier to bear. Their friend was getting older and couldn't visit them as much as he used to.

Chapter 14

A Bad Day

Bailey hadn't been for a walk in a long time. It was months since he saw his friends, any of them apart from Mark, Ben, Ma and Pop. It hurt him to walk, to go places further than the end of the drive. His hips hurt, his paws hurt and his eyes didn't work as well as they once did. He missed all of his friends, missed playing with the children he knew, making them laugh. He missed Marianne, sitting with her while she stroked his head and played with his ears. He missed Old Man Joe and the grumbling he did to himself when he was working on his projects. Bailey was sure that Axel was lonely without him too, tied up all alone in the front yard of Amos' house. He hoped that the coyotes wouldn't come back to bother the dog, he couldn't protect himself on his own. He even missed the chases he used to have with Officer Henderson.

As much as he wanted to go and see his friends he couldn't. Mark was always there, watching him and looking after him. It hurt to walk too far and most of his friends lived much further away than he could manage now. But one day he decided that it was time to go and see someone, maybe someone new but probably just an old friend. He wanted to see them, he was growing bored of seeing the house all the time and the same people even though he loved them. So when Mark went off to town to get some groceries and Ben was all wrapped up in bed taking one of his many naps Bailey quietly slipped through the long unused doggy door in the back door and disappeared into the trees.

Making his way through the trees was hard, the ground was uneven and Bailey found himself slipping and sliding everywhere. Now and then a stray root or snaring patch of vine would tangle around his legs and send him sprawling to the ground heavily. So he decided to take the roads. He didn't particularly like the roads, they smelled bad and there was almost always some loud thing traveling along them. But they were smooth and straight and easy to travel along.

He was walking down the road when he heard the rumbling of a truck in the distance. Bailey walked a little faster but every inch of his body screamed in protest. He knew the sound of the truck, he could smell it. It was Officer Henderson and Bailey knew that he wouldn't be able to get away this time. He moved to the edge of the road, the truck getting closer. He needed to get into the trees and hide until the dog catcher passed by. He glanced over his shoulder and saw the truck now, getting bigger and bigger as it got closer. But Bailey wasn't looking where he was going, his paws hit a patch of loose shale and he stumbled.

He tumbled, head over tail into the ditch that lined the side of the road. He lay there for a second, stunned. Then he whined and tried to climb to his feet. He hurt all over and there were twigs and leaves stuck in his fur. It made his skin itchy. He looked around, seeing the truck even closer now. He tried to scramble up the other side of the ditch so that he could get into the trees. The hill was too steep and he was too weak from his fall. He whined and panted, paws scrambling at the earth. His blunt claws couldn't get his footing, he could only get so far up the bank before his legs started to shake and he lost his grip tumbling back down to the bottom.

***

Officer Henderson was watching the edges of the road carefully. He hadn't seen Spirit in many months, and a small part of him missed the chases that they shared. He wouldn't tell anyone, not even Barbara, but he was a little worried by the yellow dog's absence. He was a constant feature in George's life and not having him there at least some of the time made him uneasy. He was still determined to catch Spirit one day. He was thinking about all of this as he drove, eyes peeled.

Then he caught a flash of yellow fur out of the corner of his eye, gone before it properly registered. He saw it again, off to one side of the road and he slowed down his truck. He peered out of the window, getting closer to where he saw the yellow fur. He saw him, Spirit, scrambling around in the ditch. The dog was limping slightly and George couldn't help but smirk.

"I've got you now," he said playfully, "Can't get away from me this time."

He climbed out of his truck, slowly reaching into the back for the dog catching pole. Pole in hand he walked over to the edge of the ditch and looked down. Spirit looked back up at him with a gentle whine, brown eyes wide and sad. George grinned and took a step or two closer to the edge. Spirit scrambled for the far bank, whining all of the time but he couldn't get away. George paused, scratching his head. Why wasn't the dog running? Surely this was a trick.

He decided to take his chances and slowly climbed down into the ditch with the dog, his free hand digging into the mud to help him keep his balance. Spirit whined and tried hard to get out of the ditch but he just couldn't. George paused for a second, wondering what was happening. Then he reached out with the pole and gently slipped the loop around Spirit's head to settle on the dog's neck. George tightened the loop even as Spirit's whines grew louder and he tugged at the pole. But the pulling lacked strength was feeble and half-hearted. A small pinch of guilt niggled at George's stomach but he knew it was too late to do anything now.

Slowly he got closer to Spirit, hand over hand on the pole. Finally he got his arms around the dog's neck. He felt how hard Spirit was shaking and gently patted the dog on the head.

"It's ok Spirit," he said quietly, "You gave me a good run. But every dog has his day and every dog catcher gets his dog. This is just our time."

He picked up the dog in his arms, a shock running through him as he realized how light Spirit was. He expected the dog to be much, much heavier. It was a slight struggle to get out of the ditch, the extra weight throwing Officer Henderson off balance slightly, but eventually he reached the top of the bank and carried Spirit to the back of the truck. He popped a cage door open and gently put the dog into the cage, carefully removing the loop from around his neck. The gate clicked shut. Spirit whined softly and Officer Henderson found himself reaching through the bars to gently pet the end of the dog's nose.

"You'll be ok," he said quietly.

He walked back to the front of his truck and climbed in behind the wheel. His heart was strangely heavy.

***

When Officer Henderson pulled up in front of his house Barbara was already outside. She heard the truck coming and for a moment her heart pounded with worry. George never came home in the middle of the day. Never.

"What's wrong?" she asked, her voice trembling, "Are you ok?"

"I'm fine," George said, strangely quiet, "I caught him,"

"Caught who?" she asked, following her husband around the back of the truck.

She gasped when George opened the tail gate to reveal Spirit huddled in the corner of the cage.

"Oh my god," she said. She looked to the sky apologetically and crossed herself. "Spirit…"

"He was in a ditch by the side of the road," George said, "He couldn't climb out no matter how hard he tried."

Barbara said nothing, she couldn't. Spirit was trembling and so was she. She could see the gray in his once yellow fur, the way it surrounded his snout. He looked at her with sad brown eyes and slowly crept towards the front of the cage. Barbara hesitantly reached out and slid her fingers through the bar to scratch at his ear. Spirit whined softly but leaned into the stroking. The back of her hand bumped against the latch and she stared at it for a long moment.

It would be so easy to just reach out and slip it free, to swing the door open and let Spirit loose again. It was wrong seeing him in a cage, she knew it. He was a free dog, one that roamed around where he wanted to. He shouldn't be locked up, he didn't belong there.

"I've got to take him to the pound," George said roughly, his voice gravelly. "It's where I should have taken him straight away,"

"But you didn't," she said quietly, staring at the lock still. "You brought him here. Why?"

She looked at her husband then. She saw the tears in his eyes, not quite ready to fall. His gaze wasn't on her. It was on Spirit.

"George?" she asked quietly.

George looked at her. He shrugged.

"We had a good run," he said, "I tried to catch him but he always outwitted me. I guess it couldn't last forever. We all knew it deep down. Now I'll take him to the pound. Maybe someone will come and claim him as theirs,"

"Someone will come." Barbara said firmly, nodding her head. She turned to look at Spirit. "He's too wonderful not to have an owner who loves him."

George gently placed a hand on his wife's shoulder and pulled her back. He stepped forward and closed the gate. He climbed into the front of his truck, feeling Barbara's eyes on him. She didn't wave as he turned the truck around and drove down the drive, back to the street.

He couldn't believe that he finally caught Spirit. For so long they were playing their game of cat and mouse and now he finally had the dog in the back of the truck. It felt wrong to have Spirit there, almost as though it wasn't supposed to have happened. They wouldn't have the chase anymore and George felt his throat burn at the thought. But he had a job to do and he wasn't about to let a ridiculous thing like emotions get in the way. He continued driving towards the pound.

***

"Suzie!" he shouted as he walked into the front of the pound, "Suzie, I've got another one for you!"

"You're too good at your job," Suzie said as she stepped out of the main door into the rows of cages.

George could hear the barking and whining of dogs for a moment before the young lady shut the door behind her. Silence fell over the front office once more.

"Who've you got for me this time?" Suzie asked with a sigh, "That terrier that keeps escaping from Old Lady Joan's place?"

"I've got Spirit," George said.

Suzie looked up at George sharply. She knew all about Spirit and the chases that he led Officer Henderson on. She always laughed and cheered the dog on in her mind whenever Officer Henderson moaned about one of their chases. Her heart pounded as she walked around the desk and looked at the yellow dog sitting sadly by Officer Henderson's feet.

"You're sure about this?" she asked, not meeting George's eyes, "He could always have made another miraculous escape if you like."

"Just do your job," Officer Henderson said roughly.

He thrust the lead into Suzie's surprised hands suddenly and then turned and stomped out of the office. Suzie watched him go, her mouth hanging open in shock. Eventually she turned to look at Spirit, the yellow Labrador at her feet. The dog looked right back up at her. His mouth dropped open and his tongue fell out, dangling as he panted heavily.

"Well… what are we going to do with you?" she asked Spirit quietly, "I don't suppose your owners chipped you did they? Let's go find out."

She turned and walked towards the small examination office where all the new arrivals were taken. Spirit followed behind her, walking slowly, grunting with the effort and limping. Suzie watched him follow her obediently.

"Oh sweetie," she said sadly, "No wonder you got caught at last."

Inside the room she lifted the dog on to the examination table. She was startled by how light the creature was. Most dogs his size were heavy, awkward to lift. Often they fought with her. Not Spirit. He let her pick him up and as soon as he could he took some of his weight onto his paws on the top of the table. He quietly climbed from her arms and lay on the table, head resting on his paws. He watched Suzie move about the room, his big brown eyes following every movement.

"Ok, let's get started," she said.

She moved her hands over his body with years of experience. Her body was moving on automatic, she was barely thinking about what she was doing. She trained to become a vet so that she could help animals not let the government put them down. She loved dogs, she loved to see them happy and she tried to spend as much time with them as she could. It was one of the reasons that high re-homing rate at the pound on The Hill. Whenever a dog came in she would search high and low for the dog's owners, checking every paper that she could find, searching all the missing pet sites on the internet and spreading the word however she could. Often she was able to find the dog's owners and usually she would put in a microchip if the dog didn't already have one. She never even charged for the chip, she did it quietly. It wasn't supposed to be part of her job after all.

Sometimes she couldn't find the dog's owners, no matter how hard she looked. Those times upset her the most, the idea that someone simply did not care enough about their pet to bother looking for it when it went missing often brought her close to tears. She wondered what went on in their minds. Usually she tried to find the dog a new home with someone who would love it. Many people were looking for a dog and one who was healthy and checked over by someone who knew what they were doing was appealing. Most people thought that they wanted a puppy but Suzie usually managed to bring them around to taking in an older dog, pointing out that they wouldn't need to toilet train the dog and it was usually a lot calmer than a puppy.

There were times when she just couldn't get her way and no matter how hard she tried she couldn't find the dog a new home. Sometimes it was because the dog was the 'wrong breed', too old, too worn out, or too many issues from a life of abuse and neglect. Those were the times when she was forced to put the animal down. Those days she stayed with the other dogs for as long as she could, sitting in their cages and letting them crawl all over her. She would eventually go home and cry herself to sleep.

She knew that Officer Henderson thought she was ridiculous for trying so hard to re-home the dogs, that it was unnecessary work that she was piling on to herself. He would often make jokes and snide remarks about it all. She didn't care. Dogs deserved to be loved and have a home. She was just helping them on their way. Thankfully Officer Henderson kept quiet with his opinions on the days where she put an animal down. He knew enough to leave her alone at least.

She looked at Spirit, her gloved hands stroking through his head. There was no microchip in his neck, no collar around it. His owner, wherever they were, wouldn't be easy to find. Suzie smiled. She liked a challenge and she was determined to find the person who claimed this dog as their own. Spirit looked up at her with his big brown eyes. He licked her hand gently. She smiled and rubbed his head.

There was something in Spirit's eyes, a spark and a gleam of something. Suzie realized that there was more to this particular dog than meets the eye, something unusual about him. She picked him up and set him on the floor before she led him to the pound itself. Dogs barked and yelped as they made their way down the aisle until they reached an empty cage. Suzie opened the door, leaned down to remove the leash before she straightened. Spirit looked up at her for a moment, tongue hanging out. His tail wagged and he quietly stepped into the cage. Suzie closed the door and leaned against the bars. Spirit walked to the corner of the cage and settled himself into the bed set up there. She knew then, for sure, that there was something special about this dog. He had willingly walked into the pen, he settled down quietly and now he was even going to sleep. The rest of the dogs were barking and jumping at the doors to their cages. Spirit was not a normal dog.

Suzie spun on her heel and rushed to her office. She didn't stop or look at any of the other animals. She threw herself into her chair and started pulling up site after site that she used to find dogs' owners. Her email opened up as well and she hammered in the addresses for the local news radio station and TV station. For the next few hours the office was filled with the tap tap of typing keys and the murmuring of a voice on the telephone. Suzie was determined to find Spirit's owners not matter how long it took.

***

Later that very day George was at home. He just finished his dinner. The mood in the house was somber, quiet. Barbara barely spoke to him, he barely spoke to her. Now and then she would sniff quietly and he ignored it. If a drop of water fell from his eyes he ignored that too. Then the silence was broken when the phone rang.

"I'll get it," he said roughly.

As he passed his wife he placed a hand on her shoulder and squeezed. She leaned into the touch and sobbed quietly.

"Hello?" he said when he brought the ringing phone to his ear, "George Henderson speaking."

"Officer Henderson?" a female voice said, "It's Suzie. From the pound."

"Yes Suzie," George said tiredly, "I know who you are. It's six fifteen in the evening, what do you want?"

"Umm..." she said hesitantly, "You need to get down here. Now."

George pulled the handset away from his ear and stared at it in consternation. He frowned and returned it to his ear.

"What the heck are you talking about?" he asked, "What could be so important and urgent that I need to come into work at this time of night?"

"Well you know that yellow dog you brought in?" Suzie said, "Spirit?"

"What about him?" George asked carefully. "He didn't die did he?"

Barbara appeared in the doorway, her face creased with worry. George waved her closer.

"No! No! he's fine," Suzie said quickly. George sighed in relief and smiled at Barbara, "It's just... I sort of tried to find his owners again."

"What did I tell you about doing that?" George asked angrily, "How many times have I told you not to waste your time. If people let their dogs run wild then they clearly don't care about them."

"That's the thing," Suzie said, "I spread the news everywhere, everywhere that I could think of. And I found Spirit's owners."

"So?" George asked, "What's that got to do with me coming into work?"

"Well sir..." Suzie said, "There's umm, there's like 20 people here. They're all claiming that Spirit is theirs,"

"What?" George said quietly.

The handset fell from his hand and clattered against the floor. He could hear Suzie's voice calling to him still but he stood there motionless.

There were twenty people all claiming that Spirit was their dog. And they were all at the pound at the same time. He could hear Barbara talking to Suzie. He ignored it. He spun on his heel and rushed to grab his coat. He shrugged it on and grabbed the keys to his truck. He raced through the front door, throwing it open with a heavy tug. It slammed against the wall. George ignored it. He raced to the truck and unlocked the door.

The whole time there was one thought running through George's head. Spirit had owners, he was loved, he wouldn't be put down, and he would still be around. George tried to start his truck but the clutch wouldn't catch properly. The passenger door creaked open and he stared as Barbara climbed in. She placed a hand over his hand which was still twisting and grinding on the key in the ignition.

"Take a deep breath," she instructed, looking him dead in the eye, "And focus on starting the truck."

"What are you doing here?" George asked, a little breathless.

"I'm coming with you of course," Barbara said firmly, "I care about Spirit, just like all those people at the pound do. Now stop staring at me and get driving!"

"Yes Ma'am," George said with a smile.

He twisted the key in the ignition and this time it started smoothly. He pulled out of the drive and headed away from The Hill and back towards the pound. He would get to the bottom of this. He would find Spirit's owners.

Chapter 15

Who's the Owner?

George climbed out of his truck at the pound and stood there staring. The entire parking lot was filled with cars, neat row upon row of parked vehicles in all shapes, sizes and models. It was never this full, even when they ran the re-homing event a few years before. Barbara stood beside him and put her hand in his.

"Where did all these cars come from?" she asked quietly, looking around her.

"I have no idea," George said quietly, "Suzie said there were a lot of people but I thought that she was exaggerating."

"Apparently not," Barbara said.

As if her name summoned her, Suzie appeared in the doorway. She sighed with relief when she saw George arrive. She raced down the steps and jogged over to them.

"Thank goodness you're here Officer Henderson," she said quietly, "I don't know what to do. All these people keep shouting at me and demanding to have Spirit."

"Have any of them got paperwork?" George asked.

They walked together towards the pound.

"Not that they've been able to show me," Suzie said with a shake of her head, "A lot of them have photos and stuff of Spirit. You won't believe this but he's got like 20 different names or something. Everyone calls him something different,"

"Sounds like the dog gets around," George said quietly, almost murmuring to himself.

They walked through the doors of the pound and were suddenly hit by a wall of noise. George froze and stared around him. The group of people turned as one to look at him and fell silent. There were close to 20 people in the small waiting room of the pound. They stood in small groups, some stood alone. They were all ages and all sizes. There were tall people, short people, fat people, thin people, neat and tidy people, messy people, old people and young people. George saw one young family, a little girl held in her mother's arms crying heavily and the father sat on one of the chairs with a grimace on his face.

George took a step or two into the room and suddenly everyone was talking to him at once. He held up his hands and called for silence. No one listened. He scowled and shoved through the people even as they crowded around him, trying to stop him and talk to him.

He eventually managed to break through the crowd and he made his way behind the desk of the waiting room. Everyone was still shouting at him. Barbara and Suzie were still by the entrance to the waiting room, watching him with worry on their faces.

"Alright, alright!" he shouted, "Everyone settle down!"

No one listened, they continued to shout.

"Enough!" he roared, "Every one shut up!!"

The room fell silent. Some of the people took a step or two back, away from the suddenly loud man.

"Now if I can have your attention please," George said quietly, "I would like you all to write your names down and I'll come and talk to you one by one. Everyone here is claiming that this Yellow Labrador is theirs and unless I see proper proof of ownership he isn't going home with anyone. Now, Suzie…" Suzie looked up, "Could you take everyone's name down? Barbara can you get them lined up and then show them to a seat?"

Barbara and Suzie both nodded their agreement. People looked at each other, some confused, some concerned and others simply angry. Eventually they settled down and followed Barbara's directions as she encouraged them to line up. She was smart, getting only one person from each group to wait while the others took a seat in the chairs scattered around the waiting room. Suzie stood at the desk, talking to each person one by one. She jotted down the name of the person and the name that they claimed they called Spirit by. Each one was filled out on a separate piece of paper.

"I'll go and talk to the first one," George said, taking the top sheet, "Keep taking those names and then try and find out a little more if you can,"

"Yes Boss," Suzie said with a nod before she turned back to the line of people.

George stepped around the desk and walked to the middle of the waiting room. He checked his sheet and looked up.

"Virginia and Wilson Richmond?" he read out. A couple looked up and he walked towards them. "I understand that you're claiming the Lab as yours?"

"That's right Sir," Wilson said calmly, "We saw the notice and got here as soon as we could."

"Do you have any proof that this… 'Yellow Dog' belongs to you?" George asked, "Any license papers, birth certificates, breeding deeds? Anything of that sort?"

"No, we don't," Virginia said, "But we have pictures! We have a lot of pictures of Yellow Dog and us all together,"

"I'm afraid pictures aren't proof," George said gently, "Pictures can be faked or could just be of any old dog. Unless you have documents, proving that the dog is yours I can't release him to you. Can you tell me how you came to have ownership of him at all?"

"Well I suppose…" Wilson said quietly, slowly, "I suppose we should admit that we don't really own him as such. He just appeared in our garden one day and then he kept coming back."

"So he isn't really your dog then?" George asked, a little harshly, "And I suppose that he's not really called Yellow Dog then either."

"That's just what we call him," Virginia admitted, a little reluctantly, "He didn't have a collar on when he turned up so we just came up with a name for him."

"Right," George said, nodding his head and pursing his lips. "Right."

He turned away from the Richmonds and walked into the center of the waiting room.

"Alright everyone," he called out, "Can I have your attention please?"

He didn't really need to ask for their attention. As soon as he spoke the people all turned to look at him.

"Now does anyone have proof of ownership besides pictures?" he asked. Everyone shook their heads, "I didn't think so. Now, did any one actually pay for this dog or buy it from someone else?" they all shook their heads again, "Alright, one last question. Did this dog just turn up in your garden one day and keep coming back?"

Everyone nodded. Then they looked around and seemed to realize that everyone else had the same story. Slowly looks of amazement and surprise filled their faces. George sighed and threw back his head.

"Alright, let's hear the stories," George said. "Mr. and Mrs. Brown, what happened for you?"

"Well it was amazing," Tammy said quietly, "Sammy here is autistic," she shook her little girl gently who was still crying softly, "When Champ, that's what we call him, Champ, anyway, when he appeared Sam started talking after a while when he kept coming back. Then he sort of became her dog and kept coming back, every time bringing presents for her."

"The dog helped our child too," an elderly man said, standing up, "Our grandson Cody was struggling too and then Happy appeared. We thought he'd been sent by our daughter, she passed away you see, and let him keep visiting. He played with Cody, helped him become a happier child and he's so much better now than he would have been. We thank God and Suzanne every day for sending Happy to us."

"That dog saved my Axel," A gruff, muscular, dirty looking man said sharply, standing up. "I left him tied up outside when I went on one of my jobs, long distance one, and when I came back I found that Dingbat lying on my porch, covered in blood. But it wasn't his blood, judging by the fur everywhere it was a coyote. That dog fought it and chased it off! If he hadn't a been there Axel would have been ripped to shreds."

"He saved my dog too!" the old man who kept the bees said, stepping forwards, "And me. A bear came, a big brown one, and he chased it off. He saved me, my dog and my bees. And he kept coming back to keep us all safe. He was Bear's best friend and he was almost as sad as I was when Bear died. He's my Buddy, I always had breakfast ready for him and when he stopped coming I started to get really worried. Then Marianne over there mentioned the news of a Labrador at the pound and I came right over."

"Marianne…" George said, checking his sheet. "That would be… you?"

He pointed at a woman with curly graying hair who was clutching tightly to her cardigan. She nodded.

"Alright then," he said with a slow sigh, "How do you know the dog?"

"He saved me," she said quietly, "When he first came to me I'd lost my husband a few years before. I was completely alone, drinking my life away. Then he turned up and I started to need to drink less and less. He was my Love, come to me, sent by my husband and he brought love back to me. I felt happier and whole again thanks to him."

"Alright," George said, a hint of disbelief in his voice, everyone was telling stories of how this dog, this single dog changed their lives "Anyone else got a story?"

"The dog was Sunshine for us," a man said, standing up.

Another man rose to his feet and put his arm around his waist. George noticed a look of disgust cross the faces of several people and realized who these people were. It was the gay couple that lived on The Hill, the one that most people didn't really trust or like.

"And how did he come into your life?" George asked, "Did he save you? Your boyfriend? The grandmother that lives in your attic?"

"No," the first man said laughing. "Sunshine just helped make our dog Lulu a little braver, didn't he Bob?"

"He did Charlie," the second man, Bob, said, "He got her swimming in the water. She was terrified before, everything made her jump. Thanks to Sunshine she's as brave as any other dog now and doesn't run away at the sound of the leaves rustling."

The people looked around at each other. George was just as amazed as they were. There were tears in some eyes. Suddenly there was a clattering at the door to the pound and three people rushed in.

"Is he here?" the youngest asked, "I heard you have my dog! Where is he? Is he ok?"

"What's the dog's name and do you have proof of ownership?" George asked, his voice tired. He already knew the answer.

"His name's Bailey," the young man said quickly, rummaging through his coat pocket, "And his papers are right here."

George looked at him surprised. He reached forward and took the papers from the man. He looked at them and realized that he was telling the truth. The dog was his, at least according to the paperwork.

"It's true," the older couple said as one, "Bailey is his,"

"Diane? Henry?" Marianne asked, "Mark? What the heck are you doing here?"

"I've come to get my dog," Mark snapped, "What are you doing here Marianne?"

"I came to help Love," Marianne said.

"Who's Love?" Mark asked, look of disgust and confusion on his face, "Have you been drinking again?"

"For your information young man Love is your dog," snapped Tammy, "Love is the same dog that we call Champ, that Joe calls Buddy and that Amos over there calls Dingbat. We all heard about him getting caught and wanted to come and help him,"

"I… I…" Mark stammered, "I don't understand. You all know Bailey? How?"

"It would seem that way," George said, patting Mark on the shoulder, "It looks like your Bailey has been wandering around, making new friends all over the Hill. And from the sounds of it he's been changing people's lives."

"What?" Mark asked again, looking around at everyone, "How is that possible?"

"Can we see him," Diane asked quickly, "Please?"

"Oh god," Mark said, "Yes, please. I was so worried when I got back from the hospital and Bailey wasn't there. He's too old to go exploring. He's not hurt is he?"

"Your dog is fine," George reassured him, "He just didn't have the strength to run away any more I'm afraid. Suzie'll bring him out for you in a moment."

Suzie disappeared through the back door. Mark looked around at all of these people. They started to talk among themselves as they realized that their dog would be safe and his true owner found. Laughter and tears began to roll through the room, each person sharing a different story of Bailey's adventures with them. People who were previously strangers hugged each other, held each other's hands as they told tales about the dog that changed their lives. Mark caught snippets of the stories, tail ends of the tales. He couldn't believe what he was hearing, how much one small dog meant to so many people.

A small bark drew everyone's attention and they all turned to the door that led into the pound. Suzie was there, holding Bailey in her arms. Mark rushed forwards and took him gently from her. He hugged the yellow dog tightly, petting him and whispering. He walked slowly across the waiting room. The people, all of Bailey's friends and family gathered around, petting him and whispering to him as he and Mark passed. He paused in the center of the room and everyone crowded round.

"I don't think he's going to be taking any more walks," he said softly, "And I can see that you all love him very much. So if you want to come and visit him at my house you're all more than welcome to."

The people all nodded, some with tears falling down their faces. As Mark walked out, Bailey in his arms they hugged each other and cried together, finally realizing that their beloved dog was getting old and may not live that much longer. They couldn't deny it or ignore it any more, the proof was right in front of their faces.

***

Back at Mark's home Bailey felt very happy and comfortable. It was wonderful seeing all of his friends again at the pound, even if the pound itself was scary. He had smelled the happiness on them when he was carried out and he wished that he could bounce around and play with them all like he used to. But he was too tired, his bones hurt too much so all he could do was lie quietly in Mark's arms and accept the love that they brought to him.

Mark was amazed that Bailey knew so many people. Mark would stare at Bailey for a while before turning away and shaking his head. He started to sit with Bailey, on the sofa or on the floor, and just pet him gently. He spoke to the dog about how he touched so many lives, brought so much happiness to people. The thought of all of his friends together at last made Bailey's tail wag with happiness and joy. He wanted to bark out his happiness but he couldn't, he was too tired. He slipped off to sleep in Mark's arms.

In the days that followed Bailey's friends kept coming to Mark's house. Bailey worried that he wouldn't be able to see any of his friends any more, he couldn't really walk around like he did before. But they came to him instead. At first they arrived in ones and twos but soon they were all there, people and dogs alike. The dogs all played with each other and curled up around Bailey, bathing him in kisses and licks. The people sat together, talking among themselves. Bailey could hear all of his different names mentioned.

Joe bought him bacon, just like they used to have for breakfast. The old man lowered himself down to the floor and gently fed it to Bailey, piece by piece. He was actually talking to Charlie and Bob, the two men who he always hated. They laughed among themselves while Lulu snuffled at Joe's hand and tried to steal the bacon. Joe just laughed and gave her a piece too, scratching her on the head. Bailey was happy and licked at Lulu's nose to tell her so.

Marianne arrived a little later than everyone else. She held a box of cookies in her hand which she handed to Mark without a word. Bailey was a little worried as he watched his two loved ones looking at each other. He knew that they never got along well. He whimpered gently from his place on the sofa and Marianne looked over. Her face softened and the tension was gone. She hurried to him and wrapped her arms around him, lifting him on to her lap. She sat there, petting him and feeding him cookies. Mark sat beside her and they talked about Bailey together, sharing how he changed both of their lives.

Sam and Tammy arrived, Travis was stuck at home on the sofa. Sam looked scared and Bailey whimpered again, trying to crawl over to the little girl. But Sam saw him, smiled and rushed over. She showered his face with kisses and he licked her back. He watched her showing him the flowers that she collected for him. Bob came over and asked if she wanted to go and get some more flowers for Bailey from his garden. She went with him, hand in hand, with her mother smiling and following closely behind. Bailey knew that was the first time that Sam and ever spoken to or touched a complete stranger. And now she was doing it with a smile on her face. Bailey barked softly and his tail thumped against the wooden floor.

Bailey listened and watched as his friends all sat around, talking about him and themselves. Mark was listening, his eyes widening at times. There were all sorts of tales being told, most of them were about Bailey, he could hear his name, and most of them made everyone laugh. At one point Mark led Ben into the living room and the two suffering invalids, as Ben called them, were placed on the sofa together. Mark was sad as he looked at his dad, Bailey smelled it. He could smell the disease on Ben too, the tiredness and pain that seeped from every pore. Time was running out for Ben but now Bailey wasn't worried like he was before.

Ben wasn't either. Mark had more friends now, better friends than before. They were friends that were bound by love and kindness, not by a shared interest in getting drunk and listening to music. Ben could tell that these friends would stick by Mark and support him no matter what. Ben knew that this new friendship came just in time. He was dying and there was nothing that anyone could do about it. He was worried about Mark being left alone with no one to support him and stand by him. Now he didn't have to, his friends were there and they probably always would be. Ben sighed happily and looked down at Bailey.

"You are a strange and mysterious dog Buddy," he said softly, "You've touched lives and changed them and you've brought us all together. Thank you."

Ben placed a soft kiss on Bailey's nose and then asked to be taken back to his room to go to sleep again. Charlie helped Mark lead him away.

Bailey whined and tried to stand up as Ben walked away. Marianne tried to quiet him but it didn't work. Bailey needed to go to the bathroom but he couldn't tell his friends that. He limped over to the door and scratched at it. He glanced over his shoulder at all of his friends and then turned back. Everyone rushed forward at once but Wilson got there first. He scooped Bailey up in his arms and out into the garden after Marianne opened the door for them.

Away from the view of the house he set the dog down and waited while he did his business. Then he picked Bailey up again and brought him back to the house.

Day after day the pattern was repeated. His friends would come and go at different times always bringing presents for him and as time went by presents for Mark and Ben too. They would all sit and talk and laugh and sometimes cry. Someone was always ready to carry him out to the garden to pee or poop, no one tried to avoid it and sometimes they even argued over whose turn it was, all wanting to take him out and have a few moments alone with their beloved dog.

Bailey was happier than ever. His friends knew where he was, came to see him even if the weather was bad and now they were making friends with each other. Everything that Bailey ever wanted was finally coming true. Perhaps he should have let Officer Henderson catch him sooner if this was what happened.

Chapter 16

The Dream

Virginia smiled and gently stroked Yellow Dog's head as it lay on her leg. He groaned with delight and rested his weight more heavily against her. His tail wagged, she could hear it swishing back and forth on the wooden deck. She was happy to see him, safe and happy and right beside her. She missed him.

He looked up at her, mouth hanging open and tongue hanging out. It was like he was smiling at her. Her smile widened and she scratched behind his ear. Suddenly he turned and looked towards the wood. He bolted upright and disappeared, racing towards the woods. Before he got to the woods, as he was racing through the grass of the meadow he seemed to fade away. The sun twinkled brightly for a moment and the butterflies froze in the air. For a split second silence fell over everything, nothing moved and no birds sang. Then with a rush of air the sound returned and everything began to move once more.

Virginia bolted upright in bed. She gasped and clutched at her chest. Her heart was racing and every inch of her skin was tingling. Misty suddenly licked at her face, startling her and she jolted. Her dog whined gently and Virginia reached up to gently scratch at her ears, just as she was doing to Yellow Dog in her dream. And it was a dream. But something about it felt different. Yellow Dog was trying to send her a message. She sighed and lay back down, staring at the ceiling.

Where did that dream come from? she wondered. She was in the city again. Work had picked up suddenly and both she and Wilson were working long hours, trying to keep up with everything that was happening. Even their socializing and vacations dwindled to nothing. The couple hadn't been to The Hill in many months, it had been even longer since she saw Bailey. When she last saw him he looked tired and weak. His friends, the people that he made his family, had been surrounding him and caring for him. He was in a bubble of love.

The last time that Virginia was at The Hill she didn't go to see Bailey and Mark. Ben had gotten ill again, taking a turn for the worse, and they needed peace and quiet in their house. Mark sadly turned her away when she turned up at the door with a ball for Bailey. She understood and passed on the ball for Yellow Dog and left. Ben was a lovely man and she could see the stress and worry on Mark's face. She hoped now that everything was still ok.

There was no denying that every day Yellow Dog was getting older. He was barely able to move by himself the last time that she saw him. Bailey roamed the woods and houses of The Hill for many years, spent long months and years bringing happiness to people's lives and making them better people. She knew in the back of her mind even he wouldn't be able to keep doing it forever. Eventually his visits would end and he would pass away.

But the reality was so much harder for her to bear. He was the most wonderful dog, who touched so many people's lives, and the idea of him not being in the world, after knowing him so well and finally seeing how many people he affected, made her heart break a little every time the thought came to her.

Again, as Virginia lay in the early morning sunshine pouring through the window and Misty's head lying on her chest, she wondered why Bailey appeared in her dream as he did. Dreams of Bailey were few and far between. She never dreamt of him without having thought about him during the day. Sometimes she would have a problem that needed a little extra help or a little extra thought and she would think of Bailey as she tried to calm herself down.

***

It was a few hours later, after Virginia fell back to sleep for a short while, that the dream returned to her. It was a rare day when it was the weekend and she was able to sleep in just a little longer than normal. Wilson needed to run into work and it had been him kissing her goodbye that woke her up. Now, as she munched at her breakfast in the breakfast nook, the dogs racing around the back garden, she remembered the happy mornings that passed on The Hill with Bailey racing among her dogs.

And that thought led her right back to thoughts of the dream. She still couldn't figure out why she had the dream. She wanted to know and she decided that the best way to find out was to get in touch with someone on The Hill. She was still in contact with many of the people that she met, she still emailed them once a month to talk about what was going on in their lives. The last email that she received was from Marianne and it was only a week before.

She was meaning to reply for a while and realized that this sudden need to check on Bailey was just the push that she needed to send that email. Briefly she wondered whether that was why he appeared in her dream, if it was his way of getting her to connect with her newest friends. She fired up her computer and quickly began to type an email.

Dear Marianne,

I hope all is well on The Hill. Things are still very busy here and it makes me sad that I just haven't had the chance to return again. I know that Wilson and the dogs are itching to get out there once more and run around. I find myself missing The Hill and everyone there more and more with every day that passes. Hopefully it won't be too long before we have the chance to return.

I had the weirdest dream this morning. Bailey was in it, running around with my dogs like he used to. He fought with a coyote and chased it off, like the story that Amos told us about him saving Axel. He saved my dogs' lives in my dream. I thought it was a bit strange he so rarely shows up in my dreams unless I've seen him recently when I've been on The Hill.

I suppose what I'm trying to say is how is Bailey doing? We all miss him terribly and I know that the dogs are looking forward to seeing him again.

Yours,
Virginia
Xxx

She read through what she wrote, checking it almost out of habit for any errors or spelling mistakes. There were none and after making a few corrections to some phrasing she was satisfied with the email. She hit the send button. The message was sent quickly, the whooshing sound of the computer telling Virginia that it was sent to Marianne without a hitch.

For a little while Virginia sat at the computer, refreshing her inbox over and over, just waiting for a response from her friend on The Hill. Eventually with Misty whining at her feet and Chewy scratching at the door she realized that sitting and waiting was doing nothing. She decided to take the dogs for a walk and they rushed around her as she went to fetch their leads. She missed being able to just get up and walk out of the door, it's what she could do at The Hill. But this was the City and leaving your dog off the lead was just asking for trouble.

***

There was a reply flashing on her screen when she returned from the walk. The dogs tumbled into the sitting room and piled up on top of each other in front of the empty fireplace. The moment that Virginia saw the flashing icon she rushed over and opened the message.

Virginia,

I don't know how to tell you this but Bailey isn't with us anymore. He passed away last night, at about 3am. I'm so sorry that you didn't get to see him again before he went.

There was nothing that we could do I'm afraid. Mark called in the vet around 11 in the evening, they sat on either side of Bailey, stroking him and trying to make him more comfortable. Even the vet wanted to help him pull through, it turns out that the story of Bailey's mischief and many families has spread all over The Hill. I suppose it's one of those things that happens when you live in a small town.

Anyway, I'm rambling but I think that I'm a little bit in shock if I'm honest. I'm not quite sure what's going on any more.

I know that we all knew it would have to happen eventually but it's still a shock. I can't believe that Bailey is actually gone. We tried everything that we could, Mark even turned to some of that alternative medicine but there was nothing to be done. Bailey was just too old, too worn out. He couldn't keep living any longer. We could see how much it was hurting him to keep going.

We had to have him put down, there was no other way. Bailey loved us all, very much, and I think that we all knew that he would keep going for as long as he could, even if he ended up suffering for it. So Mark and the vet agreed that it was better to just help him relax and slip away peacefully. If they hadn't he would still be in so much pain.

Mark is devastated, absolutely heartbroken. He's not been able to tell anyone. He's just lying on his side on the sofa, clutching Bailey's blanket. He's crying his heart out, bless him. I'm at their house now and I've been ringing around, telling people what's happened. You were going to be next but I wanted to tell you over the phone, not in a voicemail message. I know that you and Wilson have been working a lot of weekend hours so I was planning on calling you a little later, around lunchtime so that you would be able to actually talk to me.

I have to go now, Mark is still very upset and I've offered to look after Ben while he grieves. Ben's very upset too but he's doing much better than he was the last time that you saw him. He's able to do a bit of walking around now, even if he does need someone to lean on. But that's what friends are for after all, just like Bailey taught us all, friends are there to lean on and be leaned on by.

Again, I'm sorry that I wasn't able to tell you sooner, it all happened so quickly.

Much love and virtual hugs,

Marianne

xxxx

Virginia was shaking as she finished reading the email. Her hands came up to her mouth and she gasped for breath. A lump rose up in her throat and her eyes burned with unshed tears. He was gone, Bailey was actually gone. She felt her heart break and she stumbled across the room to collapse on to the sofa. She lay there, sobbing into a pillow for a while. The dogs gathered around her and rested their heads on various parts of her body, whining softly. They did nothing else. It was like they knew why she was so upset and were mourning with her.

Eventually the tears faded down and Virginia hovered on that line, the edge between being awake and being asleep. She realized, at that very instant, why she had that dream. She knew why Yellow Dog appeared in it, so young and free like he had once been.

Bailey was sending her a message. At the instant of his death he was sending her a message and showing her that he was ok. His spirit visited her and showed her that he was running free once more. He was exploring and racing around and having adventures like he used to do, before he grew too old. Bailey was telling her not to worry and reassuring her that he was happy and safe. He reminded her of all the times that he looked after her dogs and perhaps, he was telling her that he would continue to look after them, even now he was dead.

As Virginia lay there she wondered how many other people whose lives Bailey touched had a similar dream. How many of them saw Bailey as they slept at the moment that he slipped away? How many now knew that he was telling them that he was ok, free and happy like he had been before time had finally caught up with him? She hoped that everyone dreamed of Bailey and saw him as a young and happy dog. She hoped and prayed that they too felt his loss, just like she did, but got solace from the dreams and felt a sense of peace.

Bailey was a free spirit, he always was. He'd traveled and moved and made many new friends. He changed people's lives in ways that they never imagined and now he was gone from their world. He would never be forgotten. He touched too many people's lives for that to happen. Too many people knew him, loved him and mourned him. They would feel his loss, just as they felt his presence and they would help each other grieve and move on, remembering the good times together and always having new stories to tell.

Everyone would feel his passing just as strongly as each other. They all knew him, loved him and owned a tiny piece of him. But no one owned him completely. He wasn't Amanda's dog, he wasn't Ma and Pop's dog, he wasn't even Mark's dog despite the fact that Mark by law was the owner.

He wasn't the kind of dog that you owned. He was the kind of dog you loved and made a part of your family. He was a dog of the people, he was everyone's dog and he would be missed by everyone equally, just as he was loved by everyone equally. Even in death he would bring them closer together.

Epilogue

Not Always The End

A year went by and Bailey was still very much missed on The Hill. He wasn't forgotten and in fact his death created a new family, all of its own, tied together by their memories and tales of the yellow dog who changed their lives. They even called themselves a family, The Hill Family, and everyone who ever knew and loved Bailey, regardless of his name, was welcome to be a part of it.

It was on the anniversary of Bailey's death that they all got together once more, wherever in the world they might have been each and every family member turned around and came back home, home to The Hill. Mark was lonely since Ben passed away, he spent a lot of time rattling around the big house that they built together. It was quiet, peaceful, but still too big and empty for him on his own. So when person after person turned up on his doorstep, exactly one year to the day when Bailey left their world forever he was grateful and flung the door open. Virginia and Wilson were the last to arrive, having gotten caught up in traffic on the way out of the city and they were greeted with dozens of smiling faces.

"Hey!" Marianne cried, rushing over to wrap Virginia in a hug, "I'm so glad that you made it!"

"We almost didn't," Wilson said with a soft laugh as he hung his coat upon the hooks. "You wouldn't believe the traffic on the way up here, the roads were murder, I swear."

"One of these days you're gonna have to give up on the city," Mark said, hugging Wilson and clapping him on the back, "Do like we've done and get yourself moved out here. Best choice that I ever made."

Mark glanced briefly at Marianne and smiled. She blushed and looked away, her blush growing deeper when she caught Virginia's questioning look. She didn't respond, instead, she turned around and hurried into the den where everyone else was waiting. Virginia followed, sending a sly smile at Wilson. She stopped at the threshold and gasped. There, right in the middle of Mark's dining table, was a large picture of Bailey. In fact Virginia recognized it as one that she took herself. Beside it, slightly smaller but still fairly large, was a picture of The Hill Family, taken when they first discovered the truth about Bailey's many owners and their shared love for the dog.

The two photographs were surrounded by flowers, flowers of all different sizes and colors. There was a painted portrait of Bailey, resting in Ben's lap and Virginia guessed that it may have come from Ma. She had a vague memory of seeing the moment captured on the canvas herself but she couldn't pin it down exactly. In front of the painting, photographs and flowers were trays of bacon and cookies, separated but beautifully laid out. There was a delicate metal cage, filled with flowers. The mesh was too tightly woven to see what was inside but Virginia was sure that she caught flashes of color and the fluttering of tiny, delicate wings. She walked over and looked a little closer before she put a photo album that she'd put together on to the table top. It was filled with photographs of Bailey, both before and after they learned the truth about exactly how many people knew him. He was always doing his doggy smile, brown eyes shining.

Charlie and Bob stood to one side of the table, messing with something that was wrapped in a cloth. She walked over and hugged them both tightly, careful not to knock their package from their hands.

"So who brought all of this then?" she asked once she stepped back.

"The bacon came from Joe," Bob said, fussing with a corner of the cloth, "Of course. Bailey loved his bacon and it only seems fitting. Pop said he'd rustle up some burgers to have with it once the ceremony's done with."

"And we can have cookies for dessert," Charlie said with a grin, "Marianne brought them along. I think she may have made them herself, she had flour in her hair when she arrived."

"What's in the cage?" Virginia asked, peering at it a little closer, "I can't see in,"

"Oh that's from the Browns," Mark said, coming over to join them, "Sammy wanted to release some butterflies so apparently she and her brother have spent the last few days catching them. Travis made the cage from his seat on the sofa,"

"Is he still having back problems then?" Virginia asked sadly, "He can't get any more help?"

"We're trying all we can," Mark said, shrugging, "We've all tried. The hospital are taking him a little more seriously now that he's got a lot of people asking for their help."

"It's amazing what doctors will do sometimes," Charlie said, a little wistfully, "Especially when they come to collect a patient and find the waiting room filled with 20 other people who all want him to be treated."

"Oh you didn't!" Virginia cried,

"Oh we did," Bob said. He giggled a little maniacally. "I don't think the doctor knew whether to call security, the police or the psych ward,"

"Oh you are all evil," Virginia said sternly. She ruined it a second later by laughing.

"So boys," Old Man Joe called out as he walked over to the table, "Are you going to show us what's under the cloth now or what?"

"We've been waiting for you to get here," Bob whispered to Virginia, "And Joe is not a patient man,"

Virginia raised a hand to her mouth to stifle her giggle. Mark was talking, beckoning everyone closer and they all stood facing him and the table in a massive semi-circle.

"My friends," Mark said, "I just want to thank you all so much for coming today. I know that most of you have come in order to remember Bailey but I just want to let you all know how much it means to me to see your faces and to see all the wonderful gifts that you've all brought. It always amazes me how much love that Bailey brought into this world and into all of our lives and I would never have believed that a single dog would have brought so many people together, in love and memory, like we have here. I wouldn't believe it unless I saw it and if I'm honest, I still can't believe it."

The small group clapped and some of them shouted words of agreement. Mark raised his glass to them all and they raised up their drinks too.

"To Bailey," he said, "May we feel his love even though he is no longer with us. May his memory never fade and may his work last forever."

"To Bailey!" called out the whole group.

They toasted and took a sip of their drinks.

"And before we head outside," Mark said, "Because we do need to go outside and let free all of these lovely butterflies that Sam has brought us. Before we go outside I believe that Bob and Charlie have something to show us all. Some of us have been waiting a really long time so let's get on with it,"

"Shove out the way then," Joe called out, "And let the boys get the cloth off that thing,"

The group laughed. Bob patted Joe on the back as he passed the old man and walked to the front.

"We weren't quite sure how to remember Bailey," Charlie admitted as he looked at everyone, "I mean, we couldn't exactly give you a cut out of the sun, and yes, that's what Bob wanted to do," the group laughed quietly, "And we couldn't dig you all a pond. For one thing, it took way too long to make ours, I don't want to make another one," again the group laughed, "But then we realized something. That to us, Bailey was Sunshine, but to others he was Buddy, Dingbat, Champ, Yellow Dog and so on. He was a different dog to all of us with a different name."

"Basically what my other half is trying to say," Bob said, stepping forward, "Is that we made this for everyone, in memory of the dog with many names and so much love,"

Bob whipped off the cloth that covered the package and the room fell silent. Mark slowly stepped forward with his hand outstretched and mouth hanging open. He reached out and gently ran his fingers over the brass plate. It was cold and smooth, a rich deep orange-red color. The words etched in were filled with black and stood out starkly against the brass. He stared at it, tracing each of the letters with his fingers. He mouthed the words as he went. His fingers then moved to brush against the dark wood, smooth and well varnished, that the brass plate was attached to.

He stepped back at last and everyone could see what amazed him so much. It was a beautifully carved plaque and it was engraved with an image of Bailey's head. Around the head were words and as Virginia stepped a little closer she was able to see that those words were in fact all of the names that Bailey had gone by over the years with his Hill Family. She sobbed quietly and felt Wilson wrap his arm around her shoulders. The group were quietly whispering and murmuring to each other, sounds of agreement and a touch of sadness filled the air. It seemed that everyone agreed with the offering that Bob and Charlie were making.

"Butterflies!" Sammy cried suddenly.

Her shout made a few people jump, it was so unexpected, but they quickly began to laugh. Joe ruffled her head and then everyone began to file out of the room, and the house, heading towards Mark's large back garden. They stood in the back garden, looking around at the flowers and the trees and most of them had the same thought. Bailey would love this right now. Sam stepped forward, clutching her metal cage tightly. As the young girl passed Virginia she could hear the paper like scratches as the butterflies' wings fluttered furiously.

It was as though they were all sharing the same mind in that moment. Without being told to the group made a circle around Sam as she stood in the very center of Mark's lawn. She carefully knelt down on the ground and placed the butterfly cage in front of her. She then reached out, ever so slowly and took a hold of the lid. With one quick sweep of her arm she pulled the cage up and away. For a moment the butterflies didn't seem to know what was going on and stayed where they were. Then in a great rush of fluttering wings and a cloud of color the butterflies burst out in a great cloud and soared up into the air.

The Hill Family cricked their neck towards the sky, expecting to watch the insects fly away but instead the butterflies just spread out over the clearing that Mark's garden made in the woods and hovered in place, just a few inches above their heads. Ma reached a hand up towards them and one butterfly gently flew down to perch on the end of her finger. She laughed and drew her hand closer to her face, looking at the brightly colored wings of the delicate creature. She laughed again and the butterfly took off, rejoining its brothers and sisters in the air. Sam laughed loudly and as if it were a signal the butterflies seemed to explode and fly off in all different directions.

Eventually the butterflies had all flown away and the group stopped watching the sky and turned to each other. It was no surprise that there were tears on more than a few faces. The way that the butterflies remained for a while and then flown off, the butterfly landing on the end of Ma's finger, it all felt like it were a sign from Bailey's spirit, just like the dream from the year before. The Yellow Dog would be missed but never forgotten. He made that impossible.

***

Of course after that life continued on The Hill. Every year The Hill Family would gather together and remember the dog that united them all. They continued to share stories of Bailey and as more time passed they shared more stories about themselves.

Old Man Joe acquired more bees, building himself a few more bee hives. He no longer hated people as much as he once did, he even decided to try selling his honey at the local farmers market every week. When he needed to put up a new fence around his property, the old one having finally given into age and bad weather he was surprised when Charlie and Bob turned up to help him. They drove past and then stopped, turned around and got out of their car. There was barely a word shared between the three as the couple picked up some tools and started to help their neighbor.

That brought them closer together and within a few weeks the couple returned to help Joe build another fence and repair his cabin. After that whenever the couple went out of town they asked Joe to look after Lulu. The little dog loved her new friend and would sometimes lead Charlie to the house when they went on their walks. She always got bacon from Joe whenever they visited and he enjoyed playing with the little dog more than he ever could have imagined.

Amos continued on his road trips, driving the big rig around the country, delivering his loads and seeing old friends. But now he no longer left Axel behind, tied up in the yard. After Bailey passed away Amos started to take Axel with him, right up there in the passenger seat. He was surprised really, the journeys no longer seemed as long and he no longer felt so lonely. He always had a friend with him, no matter how far from home he was or how deserted the road seemed. In his own way Axel actually helped Amos make some better friends among his trucker brethren.

Axel loved it too. He would stick his head out of the window and let the wind blow through his fur, tongue hanging from his mouth. At the truck stops that Amos used Axel would be let out of the truck and be allowed to wander around. He made a lot of friends there, seeing all the other truck drivers and even some random ordinary people who stopped for a break from driving. He would get cuddles and strokes from strangers and sometimes even get some random bits of food. The truckers would always remember him whenever they saw him. And every night, whether they were out on the road or at home on The Hill, Amos would wrap his arms around Axel and give him a great big hug. Axel liked that part the most but he missed his old friend Dingbat.

Cody too grew and changed since Bailey passed away. He was no longer on the medication that he was on as a teenager. He was happier and felt more normal without it. He went to college and even found himself a girlfriend. He enjoyed it all, soaking up the life as a college student and making many, many friends. In his spare time he volunteered at a local animal shelter, close to wherever it was that he lived. It made him feel closer to Bailey, even though the dog was gone. He liked to help the animals find a new home, give them the love and affection that was so clearly missing in their lives. His grandparents have never been prouder of him.

The Browns were doing well too. They were still happy and filled with love for each other and Travis' back was even doing much better. The Hill Family all clubbed together to get him the help that he really needed and he was now working from home, making ornaments in his seat in the living room. He made a fair amount of money from it and every time he made a butterfly cage he was reminded of Champ and the way that he changed their lives forever. Little Sam was doing well too, she was always growing bigger and bigger and she was still talking to everyone. She talked to everyone and did very well in school. She wasn't shy any more, she wasn't afraid to be herself, she worked as hard as she could and studied hard. She was even taking painting lessons from Ma and her room was filled with paintings that she did of butterflies and dogs. Bailey always appeared in one picture she made a week.

Ma and Pop still had Shadow and were still painting and having people around. They were no longer scared to have people around, as Shadow got older he was no longer angry, or at least as angry as he was before. He even warmed up to other dogs being around him, he actually let them into the house. Ma and Pop shared stories of Bailey with their daughter Amanda and the more that she heard about The Hill Family and life on The Hill in general the more she wanted to be a part of it. She was looking for a quieter life, an easier life now that her days of hunting for a partner long over and she started to look for a house on The Hill that she could buy.

Marianne and Mark were no longer hating each other. They no longer got into shouting matches about Mark's parties and him shooting off his gun. In fact, after Ben passed away the pair spent more and more time together and grew closer. They eventually apologized to each other for all of the times that they shouted at each other and every mean word that they exchanged. More time passed and the two eventually started dating, discovering that they had more in common than they had differences. Mark of course was still hurting too much to get another dog and he deeply missed having a dog around. But by dating Marianne he was able to spend time with her dogs and although they didn't fill the hole that Bailey left behind completely, they did make him feel a little better and he enjoyed spending time with them.

Virginia and Wilson also left the city at last. They brought their dogs in from the city and lived on The Hill. They quit their jobs, finally growing tired of all of the bustle and rush of the city. The couple gathered up the Shepherd dogs into the car and set off to The Hill for the rest of their lives. They built a big barn on their land and set up some dog kennels. Remembering Bailey and how he was so upset by the pound, they began to foster rescue dogs. They worked with the pound to take in animals that weren't quite ready to be re-homed, simply because they were so badly neglected or needed more feeding up. They fostered dogs too, looked after them while their owners were away or between being adopted and going to their new homes.

Virginia was always filled with memories of Yellow Dog and couldn't get him out of her mind. She continued to take photographs, of her dogs, of her friends and of life on The Hill. Eventually she felt the need to tell the story of Yellow Dog, she wanted to share it with the world. So she started to write a book, all about Yellow Dog and the many lives that he led.

***

Officer George Henderson missed Bailey more than he thought that he would. He hadn't seen the dog since the day that his many owners were discovered but Barbara had. She went to the house with all of his owners, she continued to attend the memorial ceremonies that The Hill Family held and she remained close friends with all of them. She returned from spending time with them and shared stories with George of all of Spirit's exploits. The stories made him laugh but they also made him miss Spirit and their chases more than ever.

And then one day Suzie called him.

"Hey boss," she said brightly when he answered, "There's a situation here at the pound that I think you need to take care of."

"Please tell me it's not another twenty people all claiming to be the owner of one dog," he said with a sigh, "I don't think that I can take that again,"

"Just come in," Suzie said. Then she hung up.

On the drive over there George wondered what was going on. Suzie sounded more amused than stressed and he couldn't help but worry that she was up to something. When he got to the pound he was met by the smiling blond girl and led quietly to the office. She held a finger to her lips and then pointed at the window in the door. He peeked through it and saw a small bundle of yellow fur crouched on the table. He quietly let himself in and the bundle stirred.

He was looking at a small yellow puppy, almost exactly like Bailey looked when he was a puppy. Barbara showed George photographs that she got from Ma and Pop. The little pup looked up at him and its eyes twinkled. He had seen that look before.

He wordlessly walked over, picked the puppy up in his arms and carried her out of the office. He walked past a grinning Suzie, ignoring the giggle that came from the girl's mouth. Inside his truck he put the puppy in the front seat and climbed into the driver's seat. He glanced at her. The little dog's mouth was hanging open and her tail was wagging.

"Let's go home," he said quietly before he started the engine.

***

Barbara let herself into the house later that evening and was surprised when she saw that the lights were on. She worked late that night and was exhausted but usually, whenever she worked late she would return to a quiet house with no lights, no dinner ready and George already tucked up in bed fast asleep. Tonight George met her in the hallway and kissed her softly. He helped her out of her coat and led her into the kitchen. There was a meal set out on the table, still steaming and the entire room smelled wonderful.

Then she spotted the big box by her place setting. It was white with a few small holes dotted around. There was a big blue bow tied on top. She took a few steps closer and the box shook slightly. There was a squeaking sound coming from inside. She looked at George in question but he just smiled at her with a strange twinkle in his eyes. She undid the lid, pulling the bow apart carefully.

Almost instantly the lid popped off and a small furry head popped out. She cried out and took a step back. It was a puppy, a small Labrador, and it tumbled out of the box and on to the table. It bounced and jumped at her, yapping softly. The dog's tail wagged the entire time and eventually Barbara reached out and stroked the puppy's soft head. The puppy's entire body shook, its tail was wagging so hard, and it licked at her hand until Barbara picked it up and held it to her chest. Then the puppy licked at her face and wiggled in her arms, trying to get as close to its new owner as it could.

Barbara felt something tickling at her cheeks and when she brushed it off her fingers came away wet. She was crying. She felt like her heart would burst it was so full of love in that moment. She cried and cried and cried as she looked at the little animal in her arms. Finally she looked up at George and saw that he was smiling at her, widely. His eyes were filled with tears.

He walked over to her and wrapped his arm around her shoulders, pulling her close to his chest. His other hand gently tickled at the pup's head and received a lick too. He kissed Barbara gently on the mouth.

"You need to give her a name," he said quietly.

Barbara looked at the dog in her arms for a moment. Her mind ticked over, names rushing through. The puppy yapped and tilted her head to one side, giving a small squeaking whine as she stared right into Barbara's eyes.

"Angel," she said quietly, "We will call her Angel."

To Be Continued

Made in the USA
Middletown, DE
29 March 2017